# "Paul, Let's Pretend This Is Our Honeymoon House,"

Danielle said. "Just for tonight."

Paul swooped her up in his arms. "Like this?" He brought her back outside into the darkness. Then he carried her over the threshold, like a groom with his bride.

Danielle felt a burst of joy. "I feel like we're marr—" She stopped herself. She couldn't spoil the beautiful moment between them. She didn't want to scare him off. Not when he was feeling so close to her.

"Let's do it the right way," Paul whispered as he carried her up the winding staircase to the master bedroom....

Dear Reader,

This month we have some special treats in store for you, beginning with *Nobody's Princess*, another terrific MAN OF THE MONTH from award-winning writer Jennifer Greene. Our heroine believes she's just another run-of-the-mill kind of gal…but naturally our hero knows better. And he sets out to prove to her that he is her handsome prince…and she is his princess!

Joan Elliott Pickart's irresistible Bishop brothers are back in *Texas Glory*, the next installment of her FAMILY MEN series. And Amy Fetzer brings us her first contemporary romance, a romantic romp concerning parenthood—with a twist—in *Anybody's Dad*. Peggy Moreland's heroes are always something special, as you'll see in *A Little Texas Two-Step*, the latest in her TROUBLE IN TEXAS series.

And if you're looking for fun and frolic—and a high dose of sensuality—don't miss Patty Salier's latest, *The Honeymoon House*. If emotional and dramatic is more your cup of tea, then you'll love Kelly Jamison's *Unexpected Father*.

As always, there is something for everyone here at Silhouette Desire, where you'll find the very best contemporary romance.

Enjoy!

*Lucia Macro*

Senior Editor

Please address questions and book requests to:
Silhouette Reader Service
U.S.: 3010 Walden Ave., P.O. Box 1325, Buffalo, NY 14269
Canadian: P.O. Box 609, Fort Erie, Ont. L2A 5X3

# PATTY SALIER
# THE HONEYMOON HOUSE

SILHOUETTE *Desire*®
Published by Silhouette Books
America's Publisher of Contemporary Romance

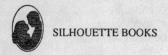

SILHOUETTE BOOKS

ISBN 0-373-76091-4

THE HONEYMOON HOUSE

Copyright © 1997 by Patty Bury Salier

**Books by Patty Salier**

Silhouette Desire

*The Sex Test* #1032
*The Honeymoon House* #1091

## PATTY SALIER

Born and raised in Gravesend, Brooklyn, in New York, Patty credits her mother for her keen logic and her father for her curious, creative mind. She has been a published writer for many years. To Patty, her wonderful husband and two great children are everything she could want in life. "I've got so much to be thankful for."

For my wonderful husband, lover and best friend,
Edward, and for my extraordinarily gifted children,
Diana and Jeff.

# One

Danielle Ford swallowed the nervous lump in her throat as she sat on the black leather sofa in Mr. Harrington's Century City office in Los Angeles.

Danielle was so anxious about the job interview that her panty hose stuck to her legs like seaweed. She yearned to remove the moist nylon and set her bare legs free.

"Danielle, the original architect I hired to design the honeymoon house I plan to build for my wife has fallen ill," began Harwood Harrington, a graying businessman in his early fifties. "Your sister, Lisa, who as you know is my real estate broker, told me that you're the perfect architect to take his place."

Danielle's stomach fluttered with excitement. "Mr. Harrington, I've got great ideas for your honeymoon house."

Did she ever! Her sister and roommate, Lisa, had told her that Mr. Harrington wanted a cozy, romantic home for his young bride, with a cute nursery for the baby he dreamed of having with her.

"May I see your portfolio, Danielle?" Mr. Harrington requested in a warm but professional tone.

Her hands were trembling. "Sure, Mr. Harrington." She anxiously handed him her portfolio, praying he'd hire her.

Mr. Harrington studied her work and frowned. "Lisa didn't tell me that you only have two houses under your architectural belt."

Danielle nervously clasped and unclasped her hands. "Yes, only two, but the owners were extremely pleased with my work. I can give you their phone numbers for references."

She suddenly felt ill. She didn't dare tell Mr. Harrington that there was a *third* house she had designed in her budding career as a junior architect.

The Tilden house had been her very first project, and a total disaster. But it wasn't all her fault. The building contractor, Paul Richards, whom she'd never met, had ruined the project for her.

She shifted nervously on the chair, feeling her panty hose bonding like glue to her skin. If Mr. Harrington found out about the catastrophe, she'd never get the job. Nobody knew except Paul Richards.

Danielle yanked at her panty hose when he wasn't looking.

Mr. Harrington leaned forward on his oak desk. "Danielle, your sister, Lisa, has gotten me terrific deals on real estate for the past few years. I owe her many favors. But I must be honest with you. I'd prefer working with an architect with denser experience."

Danielle's throat went dry. "Mr. Harrington, I've made a computer sketch of the most romantic honeymoon house you could ever dream of," she quickly said, giving her last push. "Please let me show it to you. I've got the disk right here."

As she frantically searched her black leather briefcase for the disk, the telephone rang. It was Saturday and his secretary wasn't in, so Mr. Harrington answered the phone himself.

Just as she found the disk, he hung up.

"Danielle, I've got to drive to West L.A. to resolve a business problem." He rose from his desk. "I should be back in forty-five minutes or so. Feel free to set up your architectural program on my computer. I look forward to seeing your vision of my house."

Danielle's spirits rose as he left the office. She still had a chance. She ran to his computer and inserted her disk. What he didn't know was that it wasn't just the honeymoon house job she wanted.

Her sister, Lisa, told her that Harrington was planning to build a new children's library in Santa Monica.

Danielle sucked in her breath. A children's library. She'd promised her parents, dedicated elementary-school teachers, that someday she'd design a children's library in their honor. When her mother and father were killed in an automobile accident a few years later, she'd vowed to keep her heartfelt promise to them.

That's why she had to get this job. If Mr. Harrington hired her, he'd see what a great architect she was. Then he wouldn't be able to resist hiring her as the architect for his new children's library.

Danielle's heart soared as her design of Mr. Harrington's contemporary honeymoon house appeared on the screen. As she pulled the chair closer to the computer to get a better view, her panty hose caught on a sharp edge of the desk. A huge, gaping hole appeared in her nylons.

"That's it!" she called out. "You're coming off!"

Danielle ran out to the reception area. She searched the secretary's desk for the ladies' room key. But the desk was locked.

She glanced out the office door into the fifteenth-floor hallway. The hall was deserted on that Saturday. She returned to Harrington's private office, closed his door—and realized there was no lock.

She remembered he had said he'd be back in forty-five minutes or so. She had time. So she quickly lifted her skirt and began tugging down her panty hose.

In the multilevel Century City underground parking structure, Paul Richards drove his faded green van, looking for a parking space. He was so eager to talk to Mr. Harrington that he was forty minutes early for his appointment.

He was just about to turn into a spot, when the engine sputtered and died.

"You did it again," he groaned, shaking his head. His van had stalled out on him fifteen times in the past month.

He pulled out a wrench from his construction tool belt lying on the worn passenger seat. He got out and yanked open the hood of the van, then tinkered with the valves to get the engine going again.

He needed a new van. He needed to pay his mortgage on his small cottage in Santa Monica. And he needed his general contracting business to grow, because residential building was at a record low.

At his last meeting with Mr. Harrington, Paul had handed him a business proposal. Harrington had the finances, and Paul had the construction talent. Paul hoped to create a partnership with Mr. Harrington to construct commercial buildings.

"Paul, I like your idea of a partnership," Harrington had told him. "With me as the financier, you as the general contractor and Victor Horton, the architect you recommended, we could make an unbeatable team."

If only Harrington would make his final decision, Paul wouldn't be sweating it out anymore. As he slammed down the hood of his van, he anxiously glanced at his watch, wanting to hurry up to Mr. Harrington's office.

A few minutes later, Paul quietly entered Mr. Harrington's reception area. He wished he'd dressed properly for the meeting. He'd rushed from a construction site and was sweaty in work shorts and a T-shirt.

Paul noticed that the door to Mr. Harrington's private office was closed. Mr. Harrington had told him many times to just walk in without knocking when he came by on a Saturday.

He wiped his perspiring hands on his shorts, turned the doorknob and barreled into the office.

"Mr. Harrington—" Paul's words caught in his throat.

Standing in front of him was a shapely female holding up her skirt in one hand and panty hose in the other. His gaze landed on her tanned bare legs and pink bikini panties.

"What are you doing in here?" Danielle shrieked. She yanked down her skirt. Her cheeks turned bloodred with embarrassment.

Paul leaned against the door, unable to take his eyes off her. Her black hair flowed down her shoulders like silk. "Exactly what are *you* doing in here?" he asked, glancing at the nylon hose in her hand.

She immediately stuck the panty hose in her briefcase. "I—I have some work on the computer that I need to show Mr. Harrington when he returns," she stammered. "So if you will please leave..."

"Leave?" Paul repeated, incredulous. "I'm here to see Mr. Harrington, too."

"You can wait outside."

"Are you throwing me out?"

She stared at him with bold turquoise eyes. "Listen, Mr. Whoever You Are, if you don't get out of here in three seconds, I'll—I'll—"

He was definitely intrigued. "You'll what?"

"I don't know, but I'll do something!"

Paul smiled. "I'm open to all possibilities."

"You're—you're impossible!"

Danielle felt exasperated, embarrassed, but most of all, she was frustrated at herself for being so attracted to him.

His charcoal gray eyes twinkled mischievously at her. He had curly brown hair that gave him a boyish quality. His green T-shirt hugged the hard muscles of his broad chest. She had to force her eyes away from the ample bulge in his denim shorts.

"Tell me," he began. "Who are you? I've been here hundreds of times. I definitely would've remembered you."

His steady gaze made her knees grow weak. "You first," she insisted.

No man had ever thrown her off balance the way he had. She had to sit up on the edge of the desk to steady herself.

"Okay," he began. "I'm—"

Just then, Mr. Harrington entered the office. "Paul, good to see you!"

Danielle immediately jumped off the oak desk, feeling like a complete fool. "Mr. Harrington, we were just talking."

"Danielle Ford meet Paul Richards," Mr. Harrington said. "Paul is the building contractor on my honeymoon house. And, Paul, Danielle is an architect interested in designing my house."

"Paul Richards?" she repeated, incredulous. It couldn't be. Paul Richards was the building contractor who'd ruined her first project, the Tilden house. And to top it off, he'd later given her an awful reference when a potential client of hers had inquired, even though he'd never even met her.

"Danielle Ford?" Paul asked.

The knowing twinkle in his charcoal eyes told how he obviously recognized her name.

"What a superb pleasure to meet you."

Danielle was suddenly aware of Paul's strong hand closing over hers. Though her mind fought it, she felt an electricity rush from his masculine hand through her entire body.

"Have you two ever worked together?" Mr. Harrington inquired curiously.

Danielle gulped. One word from Paul about the Tilden house, and her dreams of designing the honeymoon house and the children's library were over.

"Hmmm…now, let me see," Paul began with a teasing glint in his eyes.

She held her breath, begging him with her eyes not to say anything to Mr. Harrington about the Tilden house.

"While you two are thinking," Mr. Harrington said, "I'll take a look at Danielle's computer sketch."

As Mr. Harrington sat down at the computer to study her work, she felt panicky at not knowing what to do.

Paul leaned over to her and asked in a whisper, "You didn't tell Mr. Harrington about your botched-up job, did you?"

"*My* botched up job?" she repeated. "You were the one who constructed the house all wrong!"

"No way!" he shot back in a hushed voice. "You designed a humongous house on a tiny piece of property. Your kitchen measurements were totally out of whack, and the kitchen ended up being larger than the living room. And you forgot to draw plumbing plans, so the bathroom had no pipes!"

Her hands shot to her hips, and in a low whisper she retorted, "Really? I saw pictures of the house after your construction. The windows you installed were lopsided. The floorboard was put in crooked. Nails popped out from the drywall. Great work, Mr. Richards!"

Paul flinched as though she'd truly insulted him. "Okay, okay," he finally murmured in exasperation. "I took on too many jobs at the time. I was building three houses at once and ended up exhausted in bed for two months with pneumonia. I admit, I didn't oversee the Tilden house properly. What's your excuse?"

She nervously glanced at Mr. Harrington. Her hopes

rose as he put on his spectacles to look more closely at her design.

"I was just out of architectural school," she replied in a super-hushed voice, moving closer to Paul. "The firm that hired me was short on experienced architects. Just as I was completing the plans, the project was accidentally taken away from me before I could check for errors."

Paul's rugged face was so near that she could feel his warm breath on her cheeks. His gaze went down to her lips. For a crazy second, she felt he was mentally kissing her. And she wanted to kiss him back.

Danielle quickly stepped away from him. She could never get involved with a man she worked with ever again. Not after what had happened with her ex-boyfriend Kevin.

She forced her words out in a whisper. "If you knew the Tilden house was partly your wrongdoing, why did you give me such a poor job reference after that project? One client wouldn't hire me because of what you told her."

Paul held her eyes with his. "How could I lie about your inadequate plans?"

"You could have said it was your fault, too!"

"The client was questioning *your* architectural competence, not my workmanship."

"Lucky for you!"

"Hey—"

Mr. Harrington got up from the computer. "Paul," he said, "do you think you could work with Danielle on my house?"

"Mr. Harrington, do I have the job?" Danielle hesitantly asked, praying she'd heard right.

Mr. Harrington pointed to her computerized architectural sketch. "Your version of my honeymoon house is exactly what I have in mind. Now I need Paul's expert opinion, since he would be the one working directly with your plans."

Danielle held her breath. Paul's charged eyes were on her. Her skin grew warm. The powerful attraction she felt toward him scared her. She had to keep business and her personal feelings far, far apart with Paul.

"Let's do it," Paul said, his gaze never leaving her.

"Wonderful!" Mr. Harrington said.

She was exhilarated straight down to her toes. "Thank you, Mr. Harrington!" But as her eyes held Paul's, she felt an instant set of reservations. How could she work with him, when all she kept thinking about was how incredibly sexy he was?

"I must admit," Mr. Harrington continued. "I like the idea of my honeymoon house being planned and built by a man-woman team. However, I have one stipulation."

"Sure, Mr. Harrington," Danielle quickly said, not wanting anything to spoil her job.

"I need my architect and general contractor to work very closely on this project. The house is a gift of love to my new wife and our future family. I'd like a lot of love to go into the building of it."

Danielle's gaze mingled with Paul's. Her heart thumped in her chest. What was he thinking? Did she see an intimate glint in his expression, or was it just her fantasy?

Her voice came out shaky. "I—I have no problem with that."

"Mr. Harrington, I'm ready to start," Paul added without hesitation.

Mr. Harrington slapped his hands together. "Paul, I want a full-size trailer set up on the construction site, and I want the trees cleared off the property immediately."

Danielle was so overjoyed that she couldn't remember picking up her briefcase. "Thanks again, Mr. Harrington." Her body was bursting with joy. "I think you'll be very pleased with my work."

Mr. Harrington shook her hand. "I'm positive of it." He opened his office door for her. "Send me your entire plan. I'll make my changes, and we'll get it to the building department for approval. I want the house completed without a moment's delay."

Danielle's heart was soaring. "I'll get it to you immediately."

She practically floated out of his office. Now that she'd gotten the job, she was one step closer to talking to Mr. Harrington about his choosing her as the architect for his children's library.

However, as she got into the elevator, a sudden attack of anxiety overwhelmed her. Anxiety about working with Paul Richards.

She couldn't erase from her heart what had happened at the architectural firm where she and her ex-boyfriend Kevin had been employed. Working together had destroyed their relationship and ruined a job she'd wanted more than anything. She wasn't going to let that happen with the honeymoon house. She vowed to keep emotionally clear of Paul Richards, no matter how incredible a man he was.

Mr. Harrington closed the door to his private office and turned to Paul with a concerned look on his face. "Paul, I hired Danielle Ford because I owe her sister a huge favor. Danielle's got talent, but I don't want to see any mistakes due to inexperience."

Paul felt uneasy. He remembered the Tilden house. He couldn't afford to make even one infinitesimal error on Harrington's honeymoon house, not if he wanted that partnership with him.

"Don't worry, Mr. Harrington," Paul assured him. "The construction will go smoothly."

"I'll be honest with you, Paul," Mr. Harrington went on. "The only reason I feel comfortable with my decision is knowing you're in charge of the construction. That's why I'm asking you to monitor Danielle's work on the house."

"Watch over her work?" he asked. The idea of monitoring Danielle's plans felt totally wrong. "It's kind of an awkward situation for me, Mr. Harrington."

"I know," he replied. "But you've never worked with Danielle's plans before, have you?"

Paul anxiously looked away. He barely knew Danielle, yet he felt an immediate allegiance to her. He didn't want to risk her job with Mr. Harrington.

"I've never met her before today, Mr. Harrington," he forced himself to say. He *was* telling the truth about that.

"That's why I'm depending on you, Paul," Mr. Harrington continued. "I want my house to be flawless."

"I'll make sure of it, Mr. Harrington."

"I knew I could count on you, Paul." Mr. Harrington sat at his shiny oak desk. "By the way, I'm still intensely interested in your partnership idea."

Paul beamed with hope. "I'm glad to hear you say those words, Mr. Harrington."

"However, I want to get this project going first," Mr. Harrington went on. "I also want to discuss my new children's library with you." The telephone rang. "I definitely want you to build it, Paul. I particularly like your recommendation of Victor Horton as the architect for my new library, especially since the three of us might go into a partnership together."

Paul's spirits rose to the sun. "Victor's a creative architect. I know you'd enjoy working with him on your library."

"We'll talk more about Victor when I get my requirements for the library together," Harrington said as he picked up the phone.

Paul extended a warm, thankful hand. "I look forward to building your honeymoon house and your children's library, Mr. Harrington."

Though the partnership deal still wasn't signed, Paul knew he was on his way.

Danielle hurried into her small architectural office on Main Street in Santa Monica. She threw down her briefcase and excitedly phoned her sister, Lisa, at the real estate office.

"Lee, I got it!" Danielle gushed when she heard her sister's voice. "All because of you!"

"I knew it!" Lisa replied with joy. "Mr. Harrington loved your computer sketch, didn't he?"

"Just like you said he would." She was still spinning with joy. "To celebrate, when you get home from work tonight I'm cooking your favorite Italian dinner."

"Oh, no, I've got to work late," Lisa said, disappointed. "Then, before I leave the office, I have to phone Manny before it gets too late in New York. You'll probably be in bed when I get home."

"That's okay, Lee, we'll do it tomorrow night." Danielle knew how much Lisa looked forward to talking to her boyfriend, Manny, who had temporarily moved to New York for his job.

"I'm so happy about your new project!" Lisa added enthusiastically.

The moment Danielle hung up, she spread out her plans on the drafting table. She'd drawn a contemporary but warm two-story house in Malibu, near the ocean, with picture windows in the front facing eucalyptus, orange and lemon trees, and two large windows in the back facing a cliff overlooking the Pacific Ocean.

She made a quick list on a pad. First, she had to call a structural engineer for the framing plans. She wanted the honeymoon house to have a strong foundation because of L.A.'s earthquakes.

She also had to draw up the electrical and plumbing plans. She couldn't forget the bathroom pipes! She was so excited she could barely write.

She'd show Paul Richards she was a good architect.

Paul Richards. She fingered the plans. She knew Paul could have easily told Mr. Harrington about her part in the Tilden house catastrophe. Why hadn't he? Was he as attracted to her as she was to him?

Her stomach fluttered just thinking about working closely with Paul. The sensual way he looked at her in Mr. Harrington's office had made her momentarily forget about work.

She put down her plans and drank a cup of cold water to calm her insides. She couldn't allow her sexual attraction to Paul Richards to take over her senses. Hadn't she learned the hard way that getting involved with a man she worked with only ended in emotional disaster?

As she drank the cool water, she remembered when she'd met Kevin three years ago at the architectural firm where they'd worked together. Kevin had been self-confident and fun, and when she'd fallen in love with him, she'd shared her secret dreams with him.

She'd told Kevin she wanted to design a modern, high-tech house. She was sure a project of that magnitude would move her career ahead in their firm.

Her chance came. A wealthy client appeared in the office, seeking an architect to design his ultra-contemporary home. She excitedly told Kevin she was going to talk to the owner of their company right away and request that she be chosen for the job.

Kevin advised her to wait a little while. She listened to his advice because he loved her. He supported her. And she trusted him like family.

A few days later, she spotted Kevin talking privately with the owner. She was thrilled. She was sure he was recommending her for the job.

Then, one afternoon while Kevin was at a construction site, Danielle couldn't find her drafting pen. When she searched Kevin's drafting table for one, she felt the breath knocked out of her.

Hidden underneath other plans was Kevin's sample design of the wealthy client's modern, high-tech house and a letter to the owner of their firm requesting the prestigious job for himself.

She was crushed by his betrayal and devastated when

she found out that the owner planned to move his architectural company to Chicago and wanted to take one talented, aggressive architect along with him. Kevin made sure *he* was that architect. He gave up their love as if it never mattered, as if *she* never mattered.

Danielle crumpled the paper cup and hurled it into the trash can. She'd learned one thing from Kevin. She'd never again fall in love with a man she worked with.

The next day, after doing some final finish work on a new home, Paul sped his faded-green van toward home. He felt troubled about the idea of keeping an eye on Danielle's work. An architect had the right to privacy, and a good builder had to trust her creative judgment.

Paul made up his mind. Even though Mr. Harrington had insisted on his being a watchdog, he knew he couldn't do it. He'd make sure Mr. Harrington's house was built to perfection, but he'd never insult Danielle by interfering in her work.

Danielle Ford. She was spunky, determined and very sexy. He remembered her standing in Mr. Harrington's office with her skirt up in the air, her tantalizing legs gleaming at him and her pink bikini panties in full view. He felt his body react just thinking about her.

Just as he drove past the Santa Monica baseball field, a baseball shot into the street in front of his van. He pulled his vehicle to the curb, got out and threw the ball back to the Little League players in the field.

He watched the kids practice before their game started. A rush of warmth filled him. He loved being with kids. But he knew he could never have a family of his own. He didn't even know what being in a close family felt like.

A sadness overwhelmed him at the sight of the Little League kids' mothers beaming with pride at their sons. He'd never known his mother. She'd died when he was born. A few years later, his father had married his stepmother, who had had two children of her own, but he'd barely known his father when he passed away of cancer. Paul had been three years old.

Paul had been raised by his stepmother, who had only seemed to care about her own two children. The sole person Paul had felt close to was his best friend, Lucky. He'd run to Lucky's house whenever his stepmother screamed at him that he was always in her way. Lucky was the one who saw him cry when his stepmother told him that she wished his father had never left him to her.

When Paul had turned seventeen, he ran away for good—where nobody, even Lucky, could find him.

"Let's play ball!" the umpire called out.

The words brought Paul back to the present. He glanced at the parents cheering in the bleachers for their kids. Family life belonged to others, not him. Never him.

When Paul returned to his small, steamy cottage in Santa Monica, he pulled off his T-shirt.

He banged on his window air conditioner to get it going, but not a *whir* could be heard from the motor. Maybe with the honeymoon house job, he'd be able to buy a new one.

His stomach grumbled for dinner. He looked in his refrigerator. Empty as usual. He grabbed a clean T-shirt and headed out.

At the supermarket, Paul went straight to the frozen food aisle. He yanked open the glass door. Ice-cold air hit his bare arms. What precooked delicacy was he in the mood for?

None, he thought. Sometimes he envied the construction workers he hired who were married and went home every night to their wives and kids to share a hot dinner and loving feelings.

He couldn't remember ever having a warm family experience.

Paul pulled out a frozen lasagna dinner from the shelf and hurled it into his shopping cart. He rounded the corner on his way toward the vegetable and fruit department for his ready-made salad, when he suddenly slowed down his cart.

Standing a distance in front of him was Danielle Ford. She was bending forward, reaching into a display of ripe red tomatoes. Her tight white shorts accentuated her moon-shaped buttocks. He halted his cart, unable to take his gaze off her. Her long, bare legs winked out at him.

He squeezed the chrome of the cart handle, imagining caressing the silken flesh of her thighs and gliding his palms up to her firm buttocks.

An elderly customer accidentally banged into him with her cart, waking him up from his sexual fantasy.

At the tomato stand, Danielle lightly squeezed each tomato for the perfectly ripened ones. She was excited about cooking Lisa an Italian dinner. She had just pulled out a red winner from the middle of the stand, when suddenly several tomatoes started falling down the display.

"Oh, no!" she whispered as an avalanche of tomatoes began tumbling to her feet. She frantically pressed her body against the display to stop the onslaught.

Just as she grabbed several, a strong hand collided with hers to help stop the tomatoes. She looked up to see Paul Richards's charcoal eyes on her. The warmth of his masculine hand made her skin heat up in the icy air-conditioned produce department.

For a moment, she forgot what she was doing and backed away from the display. "Paul, what're you doing here?"

Suddenly, a huge batch of tomatoes rolled down the counter and splattered to the floor. Before answering, Paul immediately bent to catch the next batch of falling tomatoes in his open palms.

As Danielle swiftly stepped back from the counter to grab more plunging tomatoes, her foot slipped on tomato juice. She lost her balance and slammed into Paul, pushing him backward, then fell smack on top of him on the supermarket floor.

Her lips were close to his. She could feel his warm breath on her cheeks. Her breasts were crushed against his hard-muscled chest. She felt his broad palms against the small of her back. Desire raced through her veins.

Eventually, she realized that customers were trying to help them up. She rose with red-stained white shorts.

Paul's shirt was filled with tomato skins. His curly hair was moist with red juice.

"Paul, I'm sorry," she said, feeling that she was starting their working relationship on a terrible note.

Paul wiped off the skins. "Don't worry about it," he said. "Besides, I enjoyed taking a tomato bath with you."

He said it with a smile, but his voice was deep and sexy. She felt a sizzle between her legs.

She quickly grabbed her shopping cart. "I'd better pay for these items."

He eyed the food in her cart. "Some lucky guy is going to have a great dinner tonight."

"Oh, no, I'm single," she instantly replied, then frowned. Why had she told him that? Was she trying to let him know she was available? "I mean, I'm cooking dinner for my sister tonight. If it hadn't been for Lisa, I would've never had the interview with Mr. Harrington."

Paul's gaze was steady on her. "Thank her for me, too."

He turned to his shopping cart. "Well, I'd better get my Italian dinner into the microwave before it melts in the cart."

"Why don't you stick that frozen dinner into your freezer and come over and eat with us?" she heard herself ask before she knew what she was saying.

His eyes lit up. "Really? I don't want to cause more work for you."

"I owe it to you for the tomato mess," she immediately added. "Besides, I always cook way too much Italian food for me and Lisa to eat."

"When should I come over?"

Her pulse was racing. "Dinner's at seven-thirty. Here's my address." She searched for a piece of paper in her bag.

"Tell me the number. I won't forget."

"Twelve-oh-four Beethoven Street in Santa Monica," she replied, flattered and totally taken with him. "Apartment 2A."

"I'll be there."

Mesmerized, she watched Paul walk out of the supermarket toward his van, when she suddenly realized that she'd just invited the man she was going to work with to a dinner date at her apartment!

What am I doing? she thought. She had vowed to maintain a professional-only relationship with general contractor Paul Richards. Why was she giving him a personal invitation into her heart?

With a bag of groceries in her hand, she ran out to the parking lot after Paul, hoping she could make an excuse to cancel. But she caught the red taillights of his van disappearing out of the lot.

# Two

In the shower at his cottage, Paul washed the tomatoes out of his hair. He wondered if Danielle was soaping the red juice from her skin.

He couldn't stop thinking about her lying on top of him on the supermarket floor. The turquoise of her eyes. The sweet smell of her hair. Her firm breasts against his chest. Her soft body pressed against his manhood.

His loins ached.

What a glutton for punishment you are, he thought. He turned off the shower. Can't you remember what your relationship to Danielle Ford really is?

He dried his aching, naked body with the bath towel. Danielle was the architect who stood between his success or failure with Mr. Harrington. If she made one mistake on the honeymoon house that he didn't catch, goodbye partnership.

He hurried into his bedroom, zipped up his jeans and put on a clean white shirt. He glanced at the clock.

Who am I kidding? he thought. He couldn't wait to be with Danielle again. That's what scared him. He knew he wasn't destined to have a permanent relationship with her. A female friend, sure. But how could he be platonic friends with a woman as sensitive and sensual as Danielle Ford?

The doorbell rang. He buttoned his shirt and opened the door to his construction supervisor.

"Butch, you have lousy timing," he said with a grin as he shook his hand.

"I try to," Butch replied as he sauntered inside. He wore a gold earring and black motorcycle jacket and carried a helmet. He was divorced twice, with no kids and no responsibilities except to himself, and was an old-timer at building houses.

"Man, I just heard the horrendous news," Butch began. "Danielle Ford's gonna be the architect on Harrington's honeymoon house. Remember the Tilden house catastrophe? She's major bad luck for us, man."

To his surprise, Paul felt a jolt of protectiveness toward Danielle. A feeling he'd never had for a woman before.

"Don't sweat it, Butch. The honeymoon house will go up smooth as velvet."

Butch leaned on one leg and stared at him. "What's with the change in attitude toward Danielle Ford?"

Paul avoided his gaze. "What change?"

"After the Tilden mess, didn't you say you'd quit contracting before ever working with the woman's plans again?"

Paul hedged. "Yeah."

"I don't get it," Butch said, confused. "Are you *glad* she'll be working with us?"

"I didn't hire her," Paul quickly replied. "Mr. Harrington did, and I've got to make it work."

Butch shook his head. "I still don't like the idea."

Paul glanced at his watch. Seeing that it was getting late, he grabbed the bottle of Chianti off the counter, which he'd picked up on his way home.

"Hey, man, who's the hot date?" Butch asked, taking in the red wine.

Paul reached for his keys from the coffee table. "You never met her." He wasn't lying. Butch never had met Danielle.

"Falling in love, are we?" Butch added with a teasing twinkle in his eyes. "I recognize that gushy feeling when a special woman turns you on."

Paul opened the cottage door. "She's just a friend."

"Cow dung."

Paul nudged Butch out of the cottage. "Finish up the last-minute stuff on the Barry house. Then start the grading on Mr. Harrington's property and get the site prepared for construction."

Paul locked the door with an unsteady hand. Butch had hit a sensitive chord. He *did* have a gushy feeling about Danielle. He'd better curb it fast if he was planning on a platonic relationship with her.


In the kitchen of her apartment, Danielle tasted the tomato sauce in the pot, wanting it to be perfectly spiced. Would Paul Richards like it with more oregano or garlic?

She cut her thoughts short. What was she doing? She was making an Italian dinner for Lisa, not Paul. Yet he'd permeated her mind ever since she'd met him in Mr. Harrington's office.

She glanced at the small, magnetized photo of her parents on the refrigerator door. *Mom, Dad, I'm one yard closer to making my promise to you come true,* she happily thought.

That's why she couldn't let her attraction to Paul Richards interfere with her ultimate goal—the children's library.

Just then, Lisa walked into their apartment.

"Lee, I hope you're starved," Danielle said excitedly.

Lisa didn't answer. She set down her briefcase, plopped

into a chair and nervously fiddled with the breadbasket on the table.

Danielle looked at her, feeling worried. "What's wrong?"

"I was talking to Mr. Harrington's secretary on the phone today," Lisa began hesitantly.

Danielle's stomach tightened. "Did he change his mind about hiring me?"

"Not really." Lisa got up, washed her hands and began cutting tomatoes for their dinner salad.

"Tell me, Lee. I'm dying inside."

Lisa stopped chopping. "He likes your plans for his house."

Danielle suddenly felt uneasy. "But?"

"He's asked someone to oversee your work."

"What do you mean?" Danielle asked, feeling queasy. "Who did he ask?"

"His name is Paul Richards."

Danielle's legs suddenly felt weak. "But Paul is a building contractor, not an architect."

"I know, but Mr. Harrington's secretary told me that Paul Richards wants to form a partnership with him," Lisa hurriedly explained. "And Paul can't take a chance on your screwing up on the plans."

Danielle couldn't breathe. "You mean, if Paul Richards is displeased with my work, he could tell Mr. Harrington and then I'm off the job?"

"I don't know, Sis."

She couldn't believe it. She didn't want to believe it. "I knew it was a mistake."

"What?"

"I invited Paul Richards over for dinner tonight."

"Why'd you do that?"

"I bumped into him at the supermarket." Bumped? Her cheeks flamed as she thought about his hard body under her on the store floor. "He had a frozen dinner in his cart. I felt sorry for him."

Lisa's right eyebrow shot up. "Wait a minute. Is Paul Richards single and cute?"

Danielle cleared her throat. "Well, yes, he is."

"Wow!" Lisa exclaimed. "Now what're you going to do?"

"Don't worry," Danielle said in a shaky voice. "I won't get involved with him."

"But you're attracted to him, and if you work closely with him, what if—"

"I won't let that happen, that's all."

If she was so sure, why was her hand trembling as she washed the lettuce in the sink? And why did she feel crushed at learning Lisa's news about Paul?

Was it that she didn't like Paul being her watchdog on the job? She shook the water out of the lettuce, feeling anxious and upset. Or was Paul Richards already more to her than just a co-worker?

As Paul drove his van toward Danielle's street in Santa Monica, Butch's words echoed in his mind: "Falling in love, are we?"

He shook his head. How could he be falling for Danielle? He'd just met her. Besides, being in love meant sharing his life, didn't it? He had no idea how to blend his solitary existence with a woman like her.

He found himself pulling into a mini-mall at the corner of Wilshire and Barrington. He got out and walked straight into the flower shop.

*Danielle Ford is the architect on the honeymoon house and that's all,* he silently reminded himself.

The elderly saleswoman came up to him. "Are you looking for a bouquet for your girlfriend or wife?"

He shifted uncomfortably on his feet. "For a woman— I mean, a friend—I mean, a woman friend."

"I understand," she said with a knowing smile, and led him to the roses.

* * *

In her bedroom, Danielle glanced anxiously at the digital alarm clock on her bedstand. Paul was scheduled to arrive in fifteen minutes.

Her stomach felt jittery as she slipped on her silk, melon-colored dress. She fluffed her hair and lined her lips with hot-pink gloss. Though she tried convincing herself that she was getting dressed up to celebrate her new job, she knew better.

No matter how hard she denied it, Paul's coming over excited her. She knew how difficult it would be to fight her powerful attraction to him.

The telephone suddenly rang. She stared at the phone, hesitant to answer it. Was Paul canceling? She realized how disappointed she'd be if he was.

"I'll get it!" Lisa called from the living room.

Danielle heard Lisa pick up the phone. She nervously waited for her sister to say it was for her. She heard Lisa laughing and hurried into the living room.

"Who is it?" Danielle whispered.

Lisa's eyes were aglow as she mouthed, "It's Manny from New York! He misses me!"

Danielle sighed with relief. Paul was still coming. Even though she was stung by the idea that he was going to monitor her plans, her hands were perspiring just at the mere thought that he'd be at her apartment any second.

In the kitchen, she stirred the meatballs in the tomato sauce with a wooden spoon. She checked the lasagna and foil-covered garlic bread baking in the oven, wanting it to be perfect for Paul. Paul? The dinner was for Lisa, Lisa, Lisa! What was going on with her?

She boiled the water for the macaroni. You invited Paul over because it was the polite thing to do, she told herself over and over again.

Just as she put the macaroni into the pot of water, the doorbell rang. Her heart hammered. She apprehensively touched her hair and smoothed down her dress.

She glanced into the living room, hoping Lisa could

greet Paul, instead of her. But Lisa was oblivious as she whispered love words to Manny into the phone.

*I invited Paul over for good business, business, business!* she repeated in her mind.

Danielle took a deep breath and opened her apartment door. Paul's charcoal eyes lit up at the sight of her. He looked handsome in his snug jeans and white shirt with the top two buttons open, revealing his tanned chest.

She grew warm inside, totally forgetting her resolve. "Paul, you're a few minutes early."

"I couldn't wait to see y—I mean, eat your Italian dinner." He took in a whiff of air as she let him inside. "Ummm," he hummed. "Your sauce smells delicious."

His deep, gravelly voice sent a tingle across her skin as his gaze remained on her. Why did she feel he was talking about her?

She swallowed. "Make yourself at home, Paul."

From behind him, Paul pulled out a bottle of Chianti and a vibrant bouquet of yellow roses surrounded by baby's breath.

Her heart swelled. "For me?"

He shrugged, looking shy and slightly embarrassed. "I happened to pass a liquor store and flower shop."

She was thrilled. "The roses are beautiful."

She set the Chianti on the kitchen counter and slipped the sweet-scented flowers into a crystal vase.

"Paul, sit down," she invited. "I'll pull Lisa off the phone so you can meet her."

As Paul sat on a kitchen chair, his eyes never left Danielle. He watched the silk of her dress cling to her bouncing breasts and shapely hips as she left the kitchen. He swallowed and nervously tapped his fingers on the edge of the already set table.

Remember the word *platonic,* he reminded himself. Don't ever let it leave your brain.

Just then, Paul heard a loud sizzle. He turned to the

stove. White foam was overflowing from the pot with the macaroni. He jumped up and quickly turned down the flame. He picked up the wooden spoon and stirred the macaroni in the boiling water, hoping Danielle wouldn't mind.

He noticed the flowery wallpaper in her kitchen and the stack of food-stained recipe books piled on the side of the counter. Pot holders hung from a nail on the wall. A magnetized picture of an attractive elderly couple hugging was on the refrigerator door. He wondered if the people were Danielle's parents.

Like home, that's what her apartment felt to Paul. His muscles relaxed. He felt he could kick off his shoes, unbutton his shirt and let all his anxieties go.

He tasted the macaroni to see if it was ready. Not yet. He'd let it cook a few more minutes longer. His eyes caught the magnetized photo again. He pulled out a magnet from his pocket. It was in the shape of a hammer, with Richards General Contracting printed on it. He stuck his magnet on her refrigerator door.

In the living room, Danielle nudged Lisa to get off the telephone. "Paul's here!"

She glanced anxiously toward the kitchen door. She could see Paul's yellow roses beaming from the vase on the table. Her heart leaped: he was in the kitchen waiting for her!

"Manny, I love you!" Lisa moaned into the phone. "I love you!"

The moment Lisa hung up, Danielle whispered in her ear, "Don't say a word about Mr. Harrington or the honeymoon house."

Danielle knew that her sister had a tendency to open her mouth when she shouldn't, and Danielle wanted to make sure that Lisa didn't with Paul.

Before Lisa could respond, Paul stuck his head into the living room. "Dinner's ready."

"The macaroni!" Danielle rushed into the kitchen.

"Don't worry," Paul said. "Everything's taken care of."

Danielle's mouth dropped open. Paul had set the steamy macaroni in a large, flowered bowl he'd found in the cabinet. He'd put out the lasagna and garlic bread on the table, too.

Her cheeks flamed. "Paul, you're our guest. You shouldn't have—"

"Did I do it the way you want?" he asked, a bit worried.

"Perfect," she replied.

The pleased smile on his face and twinkle in his eyes made her melt inside. Why did it feel so natural having him in her apartment, when she had practically just met him?

Lisa entered the kitchen. "Paul Richards?"

Her voice had a mischievous tone that immediately bothered Danielle.

"Mr. Harrington has told me *so* much about you."

"Really?" Paul said, glancing at Danielle. "Exactly what did he say about me?"

"Well—" Lisa began.

"Lee, get the salad, will you?" Danielle immediately cut in, shooting her sister a warning look that she'd better not say a word about Paul's watchdog role in her honeymoon house plans.

Paul took it all in. "From Danielle's reaction, sounds to me like Mr. Harrington didn't give me any gold stars."

Danielle quickly took the salad bowl from her sister's hands and set it on the table. "I'm starved," she said, determined to change the subject.

Lisa gave her a secret smile and then sat at the table. "I've been waiting for this treat all day."

Danielle went to the utensil drawer to get serving spoons. She didn't want to think about Paul's relationship with Mr. Harrington. She just wanted to enjoy being with

Paul for a little while, even though she knew the feeling would end the moment they started working together.

At the kitchen counter, Danielle suddenly sensed Paul behind her.

"Danielle, did I do or say something to upset you?" he asked.

She could feel his warm breath on her hair. "No, not at all," she nervously replied.

His eyes caught hers. "Are you sure?"

For a split second, she knew he would never hurt her, that he really cared how she felt. She wished she could forget that he would be spying on her work.

"I'm positive," she told him as they sat down at the table. "Enjoy your dinner."

Lisa passed Paul the lasagna, studying him. "Paul, how well do you know Mr. Harrington?"

Danielle kicked her sister under the table to shut her up.

"A few years ago, I built a house for a friend of his," Paul explained. "Mr. Harrington liked my work and hired me on a couple of his housing projects."

"Has he ever fired an architect you've worked with?" Lisa inquired.

Danielle stopped eating. Paul looked at her worriedly. She knew he knew why Lisa was asking that question.

"Just once," Paul replied a bit uneasily. "In the middle of construction, Mr. Harrington was dissatisfied with the architect's work and hired another architect to take over the job."

Danielle suddenly felt ill. Was that going to happen to her when she worked with Paul?

Just then, Paul's beeper went off. "I'm sorry," he said as he set a slice of garlic bread on his plate. "I should've left my beeper in the van." He glanced at the number on his beeper. "Can I use your phone?"

Danielle pointed to the telephone in the living room rather than the wall phone in the kitchen. "You'll have more privacy," she said.

"Please forgive me," he said again.

In the living room, Paul dialed Butch's phone number, impatiently tapping his foot on the carpeted floor. He glanced toward the kitchen door. He'd upset Danielle by telling her about Mr. Harrington's having fired another architect. Somehow, her sister had found out that Mr. Harrington had asked him to watch over Danielle's work.

When Paul saw the anxious look on Danielle's face about the fate of her job, he wanted to draw her into his arms and tell her not to worry. He'd make sure she kept her job right to the very end, no matter what Mr. Harrington had requested of him.

When Butch's upset voice came onto the phone, Paul knew it was trouble. "Man, somebody broke onto the construction site at the Barry property," Butch said.

"Damn!" Paul muttered. "What'd they take?" He dreaded hearing. He'd wanted the Barry project to finish smoothly like all his other assignments. Why at the last moment did something horrible have to happen?

"The owners moved in half their belongings and furniture yesterday," Butch said. "The vandals cleaned them out."

Paul's jaw muscles tightened. "Jeez!"

"You want me to call the Barrys?"

"I'll tell them myself," he replied. "You contact the insurance company. Then meet me at the Barry house."

Paul hung up feeling as if his insides were about to explode. He'd made sure that the construction site had been fenced and locked. The owners had been very pleased with their remodeled house. They were planning to move in tomorrow.

Now Paul had to break the disastrous news to them. The vandalism made him feel he hadn't done an adequate enough job for them. He should have protected the property better. But how?

He heard Danielle's voice behind him.

"Paul, what's wrong?"

He turned around to find her staring at him with a concerned look on her face. Her soft voice was like a peaceful drug that soothed his insides. His agitated, frustrated feelings slowly subsided.

"Danielle, I've got problems at a construction site," he began. "I can't stay for dinner. I spoiled your great Italian meal and I'm—"

"Hungry," she finished for him. "I'll pack you some meatballs, lasagna, garlic bread and salad. You can take it along."

Before he could protest, she hurried into the kitchen, with him right behind.

The phone rang again, and he saw Lisa jump up from the kitchen table.

"It's Manny!" she said excitedly. "Paul, you're the shortest dinner guest we've ever had, but it was great meeting you!" Then she was out of the kitchen.

"Danielle, I didn't mean to mess up your evening," Paul apologized once more.

"Forget it, will you?" Danielle insisted. She packed him a scrumptious dinner in a pan with tinfoil covering. She even added a plastic spoon, fork and knife.

She handed him the hot bag. "Just like my mother used to do for me when I had late classes at architectural school."

"You're lucky," he admitted. "Nobody ever packed a lunch or dinner for me."

Danielle looked surprised. "Not even your mother?"

He felt a sudden cold void inside. "My mother died when I was a baby," he explained. "And my stepmother—she didn't have time for me."

Danielle's turquoise eyes held his, almost as though she could feel his pain.

"I'm glad to be your first time."

He felt an instant closeness to her. "Me, too."

Danielle walked him out of her apartment into the hallway. He held her warm package of food in his arms, wishing he didn't have to leave.

"Danielle, I want you to know something," he began. "You don't have to worry about your job at the honeymoon house."

"I don't?" she asked in an anxious voice. "How do you know?"

"Just trust me," he whispered.

Danielle appeared so vulnerable. Her silk-covered body was close to his. Her pink lips looked so tempting. Paul wasn't thinking. He leaned his face to hers and covered her mouth with his. Her lips tasted sweet like honey, and he wanted more.

His tongue caressed her mouth. She parted her lips, welcoming him inside. His tongue gently danced with hers and he wanted to let her know that he was with her, not against her.

He impulsively moved his body closer to hers, aching to feel her womanly curves. But the bag of food in his arms became crushed between their bodies.

Her lips formed a smile against his. He gently released his mouth from hers.

"Your dinner is steamy hot," Paul whispered, meaning more than her food.

Her turquoise eyes twinkled at him. Her cheeks flushed. He could still taste the honey of her lips.

"Don't let it get cold," she said in a shaky voice. "The meatballs, I mean."

Being close to her, nothing felt cold on his entire body. "Danielle, I wish I didn't have to go." He wanted to spend the rest of the evening with her.

"Another time," she whispered back.

He touched her cheek. "I'll see you at work."

"As soon as I get the honeymoon house plans approved by the building department."

"Yeah." He had to force himself to finally leave.

* * *

Inside her apartment, Danielle leaned against the closed door, touching her lips where Paul had kissed her. Why had she let him kiss her? Didn't he have the power to hurt her on Mr. Harrington's project? But Paul had said to trust him. Isn't that what Kevin had told her?

Lisa entered the kitchen. "You didn't tell me that Paul Richards was a hunk!" She nibbled on a slice of garlic bread. "He seems nice, too. Why don't you forget what Mr. Harrington's secretary told me?"

"I can't," Danielle said, plopping into a chair. "Why do I always pick a man whose career is entangled with mine?"

"Don't compare Paul with Kevin," Lisa advised. "I don't know why, but Paul feels honest to me." Her eyes sparkled with mischief. "In fact, if I wasn't going to marry Manny, I'd go after Paul Richards myself."

"Marry Manny?" Danielle repeated. "Did he ask you to be his wife?"

Lisa nodded, bursting with joy. "Manny's moving back to Los Angeles in a few months for our wedding!"

"Oh, Lee, what great news!"

Danielle hugged her, remembering Lisa and Manny falling in love in college when he was still living in Los Angeles. When Manny transferred to a university in New York, their love never ended. Manny had promised to come back and marry her. He'd kept his promise.

Paul Richards flashed in her mind. Could she ever risk getting close to him, when he had the power to destroy her career?

"Danielle, will you be my maid of honor?"

Lisa cut into her thoughts. A lump formed in her throat at her sister's request. "I can't wait."

"I'm calling Manny to tell him!" Lisa quickly picked up the wall phone in the kitchen.

Danielle went into their shared bedroom and closed the door to give her sister privacy. She opened the bureau drawer and pulled out her lavender nightgown.

In a few months, her sister would move out of their apartment. She'd be living alone, with no family around to share her thoughts and feelings. She loved living with her family. When her parents were killed, she'd been so thankful to still have Lisa.

You'll get used to living alone, she told herself as she stripped off her clothes in the bathroom to take a bath. Many women enjoyed living alone. But she knew she wasn't one of them. She was a family person, and she hoped to someday have a family of her own.

So far no man had felt like family to her. No man except Paul Richards. Having him at her apartment was so natural, almost as though he were living with her.

She caught her naked reflection in the bureau mirror. She wondered what it would feel to have Paul Richards's strong hands caress her breasts. Her bare nipples grew hard at the thought.

*Stop fantasizing about Paul,* she ordered herself. *Don't repeat what happened with Kevin.*

But lying in the bubbly warm bathwater, she couldn't get Paul Richards out of her mind. She visualized him climbing into the bath with her. She could almost feel his powerful masculine body sizzling against hers. She quickly turned on the cold water to startle her body back to reality.

At the burglarized construction site, Paul held in his frustration as he showed the Barrys, a young married couple, the damage inside their remodeled house. Butch began repairing the built-in drawers in their bedroom bureau that had been yanked out, scratched and thrown to the floor.

"Mr. and Mrs. Barry," Paul began, feeling at blame for the entire situation, "my company's insurance will cover everything that's been stolen. Tonight, I'll have my men spick-and-span your home until it's shiny clean. We'll even repaint the nicks in the walls and have the new carpeting steam-washed. Whatever you want. You just tell me."

When Paul saw a hopeful smile on their faces, his muscles relaxed a little. Though burglaries occasionally happened on construction sites, Paul hated seeing his customers unhappy. He guaranteed superior construction and worked on their houses as if they were his own. His goal was for his customers to move into their new or remodeled homes totally satisfied with his work.

When the owners left, Paul put on his leather tool belt and joined Butch and two laborers to make the house brand-new again.

At three o'clock in the morning, an exhausted-but-satisfied Paul finished painting and cleaning up. As he packed his tools into his van, his mind drifted to Danielle. He wished he could have stayed at her apartment longer.

Butch put on his motorcycle helmet. "Going back to your new lady's place?"

Paul climbed into his van. His normal reaction to Butch would have been an easy no. He liked his independence. He didn't need to feel connected to anyone. But with Danielle, he was aware of a yearning that he didn't quite understand.

"I'm going home, Butch." He started up the van's engine, relieved that it didn't sputter out.

Paul drove toward his Santa Monica apartment, knowing he needed to get some sleep, but he found himself diverting his route a few blocks and ending up on Danielle's street.

He slowed his van as he neared her apartment building. He stopped at the curb a few yards away from her complex and turned off the engine. Her apartment on the second floor had a small balcony. The Monterey pines somewhat blocked his view.

His heart quickened when he noticed that her living room lights were still burning. Her glass balcony door was open, letting in the summer evening's cool breeze.

He wondered how late he would have stayed at her apartment if he hadn't been forced to leave. He felt the sudden urge to ring her doorbell and ask if he could come in for a little while.

Paul knew he was thinking crazy. He regained his senses and was just about to start up his van, when Danielle appeared at her balcony door.

# Three

Paul's fingers froze on the ignition key as he watched Danielle walk over to the railing and look up at the star-filled sky.

Through the trees, he could see that she was wearing a flimsy nightgown. The light from the living room filtered through the fabric. Her breasts jutted out against the material, and he could barely see her nipples protruding.

Paul held his breath. He forgot he was in his van, parked on her street. He was aware only of Danielle's naked hourglass form silhouetted under her nightie.

His hands were perspiring as he held the steering wheel. He slowly opened the van window to let in more air so he could breathe. His body became wide-awake.

Just then, Danielle leaned over the railing and peered down at the street. Paul's heart hammered against his ribs. He was invading her privacy. He hoped she didn't see his van through the Monterey pines lining the sidewalk.

* * *

On her balcony, Danielle stretched her body and breathed in the sweet, pine-scented evening air. Then she went back into her apartment, locked the balcony door and leaned against the glass door.

Was that Paul's van she'd seen in the shadows of the pines and the streetlights? Her skin tingled under her nightgown at the thought that he might have been watching her.

*What a crazy idea,* she silently told herself as she drew the white curtains across the balcony door. Why would Paul Richards be parked outside her apartment at four in the morning, watching her? Was this just another of a zillion fantasies she was having about him?

She went to the refrigerator and poured herself a glass of cold orange juice to cool her heated body. Paul Richards had been permeating her mind all evening. That's why she couldn't sleep and had gone out on the balcony. No wonder she thought she'd seen his van parked under the trees, as he admired her from afar.

When she put back the orange juice, she noticed the hammer magnet Paul had left on the refrigerator door. Why had he put his magnet on her door? Did he feel as close to her as she felt to him? She gently touched the metal, as though caressing him.

She quickly brushed away her sensual thoughts and returned to her bedroom, where Lisa was lightly snoring. She quietly climbed into her twin bed.

As she lay on her back, she felt an aching in the tender area between her legs. She couldn't get rid of the vision of Paul watching her standing in her nightgown on the balcony.

She closed her eyes and pictured Paul's warm palm snuggled between her thighs, caressing her to ultimate pleasure. She didn't remember falling asleep.

At her architectural office, Danielle anxiously checked the coffeemaker to see if her mocha java brew was ready. Her plans for Mr. Harrington's honeymoon house had been approved by the building department, but she had a couple of small revisions she wanted to discuss with him. A meeting had been arranged for that morning.

She set up two chairs at her petite conference table. She constantly shifted them to get the perfect angle to talk to Mr. Harrington. She glanced at the digital clock on her desk. He was expected at any moment.

She couldn't wait to tell him about her new ideas for the interior of his house. She flipped through the spec sheets she'd written designating the specific details, such as white metal windows, recessed lighting, a marble floor in the entry, thick beige carpeting upstairs in the master bedroom and plenty of custom-made closets. She'd listed high-quality everything.

She knew that the more she pleased Mr. Harrington with her work the closer she came to asking him if he could select her as the architect for his children's library.

The loud knock on her office door startled her. She held her breath and excitedly opened the door.

"Mr. Harrington, I—" Her words caught in her throat when she saw Paul Richards standing there. "Paul, what are you doing here?"

"Am I late?" he asked, looking a bit concerned. His muscular arms were filled with folders and papers that were about to spew out on the floor.

She leaned out the door frame. "Where's Mr. Harrington?"

"Didn't you get his message?"

"No," she replied, panicking.

As Paul struggled to balance the stack of materials, she glanced at her answering machine. The message light was blinking. She'd been so nervous and excited about her meeting that she'd forgotten to check her machine.

"Mr. Harrington had an emergency out-of-town business meeting."

She felt totally thrown off balance. "Does he want to reschedule the meeting?" She needed to keep the momentum going with Mr. Harrington so he'd see how prompt and efficient she was.

Paul grabbed a couple of papers that almost fell to the floor. "He sent me in his place."

She stared at Paul in disbelief. "*You're* going to sit in for him?"

"I hope you don't mind."

She nervously clasped and unclasped her hands. "No, no, it's fine." But it wasn't fine. She needed to show her architectural talents to Mr. Harrington, not Paul.

Her stomach knotted. She knew why Paul had been sent. He was there to guarantee that she didn't make any mistakes. Mr. Harrington still didn't completely trust her abilities.

Paul's muscular arms strained from the weight of the folders. "Is there anywhere I can set these down?"

"Oh, sure. Right here."

As she moved behind him in the tiny space to get to the conference table, her breasts brushed against his broad back. A hot sensation rushed up her legs.

As Paul put down the folders, her eyes met his. He'd felt the electricity, too. How was she going to have a serious meeting when her mind was ensconced in her fantasies about Paul?

Just then, her telephone rang, jolting her out of her momentary sensual reverie about Paul. "I—I'll be right back," she stammered.

When she picked up the phone, Mr. Harrington was on the other end.

"Danielle, please forgive my last-minute change of plans," he said. "I'm sure you'll have no problem working closely with Paul."

"Of course I won't, Mr. Harrington."

She glanced at Paul, who was sitting in a chair, sorting out papers on his lap. His royal-blue T-shirt hugged the muscles of his massive chest. His broad shoulders ached to be touched. His long legs were spread, and his powerful, muscular thighs glared out at her.

She quickly turned away from him, unable to think straight.

"Danielle, I told Paul my ideas for the master bedroom," continued Mr. Harrington. "Please go over every detail with him. He's aware of exactly what I like and may make a couple of suggestions of his own."

"Mr. Harrington, when can I discuss the information with you?" she asked, needing to create a working relationship with him directly.

"Don't worry. I'll be in touch with you later in the day."

"Sure," she said disappointedly. "You'll be pleased with the results of my meeting with Paul."

Danielle's hands felt cold as she hung up the phone. She'd wanted so badly to show Mr. Harrington how creative and competent she was.

"Is everything straightened out?" Paul asked, concerned.

"I think so," she replied, feeling upset.

Paul walked over to her. "I'm sorry Mr. Harrington sent me over. I know you'd prefer working with him."

Paul's sensitivity to her feelings surprised her. "Why don't we get to work?" she suggested, wanting to smooth things over. "I'm going to need a few more weeks to finish the spec sheets and make a few revisions on the approved framing plans."

"Fine," Paul said. "I'll start framing when you give me those changes."

She spread out her floor plan on the conference table. "Here's the location of the master bedroom and master bath. As you'll notice, I drew two large bedroom windows facing the Pacific Ocean."

Paul shook his head. "I don't think there should be two windows."

She stared at him. "What're you talking about? I'm putting in two windows."

Paul spread his hand across the air. "I see floor-to-ceiling glass facing the blue sea."

"Absolutely not!" she protested. "Mr. Harrington and his wife need privacy for when they—they—"

"Make love?" he added in a husky voice.

His charcoal eyes melted into hers, and she couldn't think about her work anymore.

She bolted from her chair. "I'll get us some coffee."

At the coffeemaker, she could barely concentrate on pouring the brew into two cups. How could she work when Paul kept reminding her of how much she needed and wanted a man—that man being him!

Paul walked up behind her. He rested his large hand on the wall beside her. Her fingers trembled as she poured the coffee.

"Danielle, I didn't mean to make you uncomfortable."

She turned and looked up at him. He was inches from her. She could feel the heat radiating from his body.

"I need this project to go smoothly, Paul."

His eyes drowned in hers. "Danielle, I have the same need as you do."

Stop fantasizing about kissing him! she silently shouted at herself.

"Paul, you've already established your working relationship with Mr. Harrington," she added in an unsteady voice. Her entire being was concentrated on how physically close he was to her. "I want to create a good rapport with him, too."

"You will," he said with confidence. "I'll make sure of it."

He gently touched her cheek. With his thumb, he outlined the curve of her lips.

She parted her lips to his touch. "Paul, I don't know how we're going to get any work done—"

His mouth covered hers. She didn't resist—she couldn't.

She slipped her arms around his neck and pressed her body to his. She wanted to get closer to him, so much closer.

She felt his hand slip under her top and cup her bra-covered breasts. She gasped as he squeezed her womanly mounds. She ached for him to unclasp her bra and fondle her naked flesh.

Just as he reached the clasp, his beeper went off. She was immediately aware of being in her office. At a meeting. A meeting for Mr. Harrington.

She slipped free of Paul's arms. "You'd better make your call." She quickly straightened her clothes, went to the conference table and stared blindly at her plans.

As he dialed the phone number, Danielle realized that she'd never be able to have a normal business relationship with Paul. When she was alone with him, all she could think about was being in his arms.

Paul got off the phone. "I need to go to the construction site."

"What about Mr. Harrington's specifications?" she asked a bit worriedly. She'd promised Mr. Harrington that she'd get his ideas from Paul.

"How about if I leave the notes with you?" he suggested.

"But he wants your input."

"You can call me at the construction trailer if you have any questions."

"Okay, sure," she said, somewhat uneasy.

"You'll do a better job without me around," Paul added, responding to the worried look in her eyes. He headed for the door and then stopped. "By the way. You're right. Two windows in the master bedroom would be much better." Then he left.

Danielle watched Paul walk to his van. She wanted to call him back. She needed to tell him that she felt a closeness with him that she'd never felt with a man before, not even with Kevin. But she was afraid to trust her feelings.

Not yet. Not until she knew for sure that her growing

relationship with Paul was separate from the honeymoon house project. Then and only then would she ever give herself to him and take whatever he wanted to offer of his heart.

At the construction site, the cement truck roared as wet gobs of gray cement flowed out of the cylinder into a bin. Paul yelled over the din for Butch and the laborers to move fast as they poured the foundation of the honeymoon house.

Paul pulled off his T-shirt as the hot L.A. sun bore down on his bare shoulders and back. He walked around the foundation, checking every footing according to the structural engineer's plans, which were in his hand.

As he stood in the muddied backyard, he glanced over the cliff overlooking the teal-green Pacific Ocean. Mr. Harrington's property stood several hundred feet above Malibu Beach.

Paul could hear the muted sound of the crashing waves down below. Danielle flashed in his mind. He'd had no right kissing or caressing her at her office. He was supposed to be there to work for Mr. Harrington, not be intimate with her.

But when he was near her, he wanted to touch her, hold her and, yes, make love to her.

In the distance across the vast sea, he could see the outline of Catalina Island. For a second, he didn't hear the roar of the cement truck anymore.

In his mind, he was lying on a sandy beach with Danielle in his arms. He was kissing her honey lips and running his fingers through her black satin hair. She smiled up at him with her twinkling turquoise eyes. His heart swelled. He wanted to tell Danielle something—something he'd never told any other woman in his life. He whispered in his fantasy, "Danielle, I—"

"Hey, man!"

Butch's voice pounded at the background of his mind.

"Mr. Harrington's here to see you!"

Paul was jolted back to reality. "Mr. Harrington? Yeah, okay. I'm coming."

What was he about to say to Danielle in his daydream? Was he going to tell her that he lov—

"How was your meeting with Danielle?" Mr. Harrington asked.

Paul immediately noticed the frown on the man's face and sensed he was displeased about something. "The meeting went well." How could he tell him that he'd cupped Danielle's breasts in his hands and tasted her sweet lips?

In silence, Mr. Harrington walked to the back of his property and peered over the cliff at the sparkling ocean. Paul knew something was very wrong.

Harrington turned. "Paul, I thought you said you never worked with Danielle Ford before?"

Paul felt as though a pair of metal knuckles had jammed his stomach. "I—I never have, Mr. Harrington."

"I heard differently," he said with troubled eyes. "I found out that she designed a house that was an abominable failure. A house that went sky-high over budget."

Paul clenched his jaw. "That was three years ago, Mr. Harrington. I only worked with her plans, not with her. She was a neophyte architect then."

"Why didn't you tell me before I hired her?"

"Everybody makes mistakes at the beginning of a career," he hurriedly said. "I figured Danielle learned from hers."

Worry creases formed on Mr. Harrington's face. "Paul, I don't like construction delays. I don't like budget overflow. I want sharp, competent work on my house. I must let Danielle go."

Hot blood rushed to Paul's face. "You can't fire Danielle."

"Why not?" Mr. Harrington questioned. "Danielle Ford came to me under false pretenses."

"I was the one in the wrong by not telling you," Paul immediately added. "Please give her a chance to prove her abilities. She's a talented architect."

"I don't have the time or the money to risk, Paul," Harrington said in a concerned voice. "Has your architect, Victor Horton, regained his health yet?"

"I haven't spoken to him recently." Paul had talked to Victor once right after he'd fallen ill.

"Can you get him on the trailer phone for me?" Harrington requested.

Paul's mind was reeling. He couldn't hurt Danielle. He'd promised that her job was secure. But most of all, he wanted to keep her on the project because he needed to be close to her.

"Mr. Harrington, you like Danielle's design, don't you?" he quickly asked.

"Yes, very much so."

"If you switch architects, your floor plans will change. Victor Horton has a totally different style. Your house will be drastically altered. And it will take time for Victor to draw up new plans, which will cost you more money in the end."

Mr. Harrington silently stared at the ocean. His face seemed to age by the minute.

"You're absolutely correct, Paul. I'm panicking because I always look for perfection. I should stick with the plans I have." He faced Paul. "However, I must warn you. If my house goes over budget because of Danielle Ford, my financial plans for the children's library will be affected—and so will our partnership."

Paul swallowed hard. He knew if Danielle failed him, he was sunk.

"I take full responsibility for your honeymoon house," Paul said. "If it isn't built exactly the way you envision, I'll be completely accountable."

"Fair deal, Paul."

Paul firmly shook Mr. Harrington's hand on it. But his

insides were as tight as a ball. Had he lost a screw? Why was he risking his entire business future with Mr. Harrington for Danielle?

Mr. Harrington headed for his black Mercedes. "Paul, when do you start framing?"

"I've got the approved plans right here," Paul replied, hurrying to retrieve them from the construction trailer. He showed Danielle's framing blueprint to him. "However, Danielle mentioned that she needed a couple of more weeks to make some changes."

"I don't want any delays, Paul," Mr. Harrington insisted. "Start the framing immediately after the foundation is completed."

Paul felt torn. "But as the architect, Danielle should approve—"

Mr. Harrington tapped his finger on the blueprint. "These plans are ready to go. You've been framing houses for years, Paul. Use this plan and add your instinct and experience." Without waiting for Paul's response, he got into his car and took off, leaving a cloud of dust behind him.

Paul's forehead was throbbing. What the hell am I doing? he thought. I just put my future business with Mr. Harrington on the line because of Danielle. He prayed that he hadn't made the biggest mistake of his career.

A couple of weeks later, Danielle sat at her drafting table in her office. Feeling totally satisfied, she put down her pen. She'd finally finished with the framing changes she wanted to make to the honeymoon house that wouldn't involve another approval by the building department.

She'd been so busy working day and night on the spec sheets and revisions that she'd barely noticed a few weeks had gone by since Paul's intimate visit to her office.

She had deliberately kept away from the construction site because of the powerful effect Paul had on her. She knew she wouldn't get any work done with him near.

She'd gotten a couple of messages on her office answering machine from Paul about his needing her revised plans right away. She'd intentionally returned his calls after work hours, leaving a message on the answering machine in the construction trailer that she'd get the revisions to him as soon as she could.

She didn't dare talk directly to Paul or meet alone with him again. She was determined to remain focused on making Mr. Harrington's house plans better than perfect.

She wiped the sweat beads from her upper lip and turned her portable fan to high. The Santa Ana winds that were sweeping Los Angeles had made the temperature soar to one hundred. And the building's air-conditioning was on the blink.

She had come to the office wearing white short-shorts, a halter top and leather sandals to keep cool. She wouldn't have dared dress so skimpily for work if she'd had any meetings scheduled.

Just then, her telephone rang. For a second, she hoped it was Paul. She couldn't wait to tell him that she'd finished the revised framing plan.

"Danielle Ford?" an unfamiliar male voice asked. "This is Butch at the Harrington honeymoon house. I'm Paul Richards's construction supervisor. I've got a framing question for you."

"Framing?" she repeated, confused. She tightened her grip on the receiver. "Nobody informed me that framing had started. Please put Paul Richards on."

"No can do," Butch replied. "Paul's at a private meeting in Mr. Harrington's office in Century City. I don't want to disturb him. He should be back here soon, but I need an answer pronto."

"I'll be right over." She slammed down the phone angrily. *How dare Paul Richards start framing without telling me!* she thought. She grabbed her revised blueprints and ran out of her office.

As she sped in her car to the site in Malibu, she remem-

bered Paul's phone messages about wanting her revised
plans right away. Why hadn't he waited? She slowly realized why.

Paul wanted to show Mr. Harrington that he was in total
control of the construction schedule, even if it meant going
ahead with framing without her approval.

Disappointment filled her as she drove along the Pacific
Coast Highway to Malibu. She had wanted Paul to be different from Kevin. She had hoped Paul would care about
her first and the job second. But maybe he was only out
for himself, just as Kevin had been. Hadn't she warned
herself not to get emotionally involved with Paul?

She pulled into the dirt-filled parking lot near the construction site. Her heartbeat quickened when she spotted
Paul's faded-green van. Keep your heart out of it, she
warned herself. That's what he's doing!

She stuck the rolled-up blueprints under her arm and
barreled over to the site, ready to start a war. But when
she saw the wooden skeleton of the first floor already up,
her breath was knocked away.

The smell of fresh wood framing filled the air. An ex-
hilarating feeling rushed through her seeing her vision of
the honeymoon house coming to life. The floor, wall and
ceiling of the foyer, sunken living room, study, kitchen
and half bathroom were already framed.

She spotted a group of laborers pounding nails into
beams. "Butch?" she called out.

"Hey, Danielle!" A perspiring man in shorts, T-shirt
and earring appeared. "I called you back, but you'd already left. I straightened out the measurement problem
with Paul."

"With *Paul?*" she repeated, her blood pressure soaring.
"*I'm* the architect, not Paul!" She angrily unrolled her
blueprints on the dirt ground. "Show me what you did to
my plans."

Inside the construction trailer, Paul thought he heard
Danielle's voice rising in the distance. The windows were

closed because of the air-conditioning, so he couldn't be sure.

He hurriedly put aside the payroll checks he was writing for his crew and opened the door. The Santa Ana wind hit his bare chest like an oven.

"Butch, what's the problem?" Paul yelled over the sawing and hammering of his workers.

"*You're* the problem!" he heard Danielle shout as she rushed toward him carrying her blueprints.

He sucked in his breath when she came into view. Her jet-black hair was pulled back in a ponytail. Her breasts bounced freely under the red halter top. Her white short-shorts hugged her curvy hips, and her luscious satiny thighs glistened in the sunlight.

He forced his mind back to work. "Danielle, I know you're upset because I—"

Her turquoise eyes were on fire. "How dare you start framing without me?"

"Listen, Danielle, I got orders from Mr. Harrington to begin immediately."

Her facial expression dropped. "That's not fair. As the architect, I have a right to know every stage of construction."

He clenched his jaw, knowing she was hurt. "Yes, you do. I know you do." It was his fault. He should have told her about Mr. Harrington's orders, but he hadn't wanted to hurt her. He felt caught between protecting her job and saving his future deal with Mr. Harrington.

Butch walked over. "Paul, we're ready to start framing the second floor."

"Sure, Butch."

"The second floor?" Danielle protested. "You haven't gone over the second-level plans with me yet!"

Paul felt torn, because Mr. Harrington had been on the site every day telling him to move quickly without any delays. "Butch, I'll talk to you in a sec."

Butch gave him an "I knew this would happen with Danielle Ford" look and went back to work.

"Danielle, calm down, will you?" Paul said. "Your second-floor plans are perfect. Why waste time going over every single detail?"

"I made revisions, remember?" she reminded him. "And I won't let you ruin my plans the way you did with the Tilden house!"

"Now, wait just a minute—"

Danielle abruptly headed toward her car.

"Danielle, where are you going?" he called, rushing after her. "Let's talk about this."

As she yanked open the car door and bent in to get something from the back seat, Paul caught sight of her white short-shorts slowly rising up the creamy flesh of her buttocks.

His manhood came alert. *Stop looking at her!* he ordered himself, and quickly averted his eyes. He kicked the dirt on the ground with his work boot, angry at himself for hurting her and wanting her both at the same time.

In the back seat of her car, Danielle grabbed her briefcase, stack of blueprints and spec sheets. *I'm not letting Paul Richards take control of my job!* she thought. If she did, she'd never prove her talents to Mr. Harrington. And she'd never get the children's library job.

Danielle cradled her plans and specs in her arms and kicked the car door closed.

"You're not getting rid of me, Paul Richards," she blurted.

His charcoal eyes locked with hers. "Danielle, believe me, I don't want to."

She noticed that his voice was filled with emotion. His curly brown hair was mixed with wood shavings. When he leaned his weight on one leg, his construction tools jangled from his leather tool belt.

For a second, she could barely remember her anger

about the framing. She was conscious only of Paul and the caring feelings welling inside her.

Paul's gaze drifted down to the materials in her hands. "Where are you going with all that stuff?"

She pulled the plans and specs against her chest. "I'm setting up office in the construction trailer."

"You're what?"

"You heard me." She boldly headed toward the trailer, her legs trembling a little.

"You can't do that!" Paul protested, following her. "The trailer is for me and my crew."

"Oh, really?" She bolted up the five steps to the door. "Not anymore."

Her arms piled high with house plans, she struggled to open the door.

Paul squeezed in front of her. "Let me get it."

"I can do it myself!"

Not listening to her, Paul pressed his body against hers as he twisted the doorknob. She smelled his maleness. She felt his muscular chest leaning against her arm. Her limbs suddenly felt like putty. She wanted to drop the house plans and fall into his arms.

The moment he got the door open, she rushed past him inside. The small trailer was ice-cold, mildewed and dusty. There was a worn plaid sofa, a long wooden table with chairs, a tiny kitchenette and bathroom and, at the back, a small bedroom with an unmade bed.

She quickly set down her stuff on the table, which was piled with paperwork.

"Hold on," Paul protested. "That's *my* desk!"

"There's tons of room for the two of us," she insisted.

She immediately turned off the air conditioner, opened the windows to let in fresh air and began straightening the clutter.

Paul stood there nervously tapping his fingers on the wall. "What're you doing?"

"I'm organizing," she replied. "I can't work in this disoriented environment."

"How am I going to find anything?"

"Just ask me. I'll tell you where everything is." She sat down and spread her framing blueprints across the table. "I'll work here every day from early morning to early evening until the house is finished."

Paul anxiously ran his fingers through his hair. "Why are you doing this? If there's a problem on the site, I'll call you at your office."

"The way you did when you started framing without me?"

"Danielle, I wish I could say the right words to express how sorry I am," he apologized, struggling for words. "But you're being downright impulsive moving your office in here."

She angrily stood up and glared at him. "It's okay if *you* monitor every detail of my work, but it's not okay if I do the same to you, is that it?"

"I didn't say that."

"That's what you meant!"

Suddenly, there was a rumble like that of an underground railroad train approaching. The trailer started to shake. The door rattled. The plans fell to the floor. Dishes and glasses in the kitchenette jingled.

"An earthquake!" Danielle screamed, terrified of the ground moving under her feet.

Without thinking, she flew into Paul's arms for comfort. He held on to her tightly as another jolt swayed the trailer. A stronger jolt pushed her back against the trailer wall, with Paul's body pressed to hers.

Trembling with fright, she circled her arms tightly around his neck and buried her face in his bare chest. Her lips mingled with the soft, dark hairs on his warm skin. She felt his steel-hard thighs against her bare legs. His tools pressed against her abdomen. He pulled her closer, as though he wanted to protect her, as though he wanted to take care of her.

As quickly as it had started, the earth stopped shaking. The trailer was dead still. Danielle looked up at Paul. Her arms were still locked around his neck. Her breasts were crushed against his hard chest. She could feel his warm breath on her face.

Her breathing quickened. She knew she should pull out of his arms, but she couldn't. She didn't want to. She felt safe, protected, secure.

When Paul's mouth neared hers, Danielle lost all reason. She stood on her tiptoes and met his sensual lips with her own.

# Four

Paul forgot he was in the trailer. He forgot he was at work. He was only aware of his intense need to be close to Danielle. He slid his palms up and down her bare back. His fingers landed on the string of her red halter top.

As he kissed and tasted her, he untied the knot. Her halter came loose and fell to the floor. He cupped her throbbing mounds in his palms. She moaned against his lips. He squeezed her flesh, feeling her nipples harden against his palms. He circled his thumbs around her taut nipples.

She gently bit his lip in pleasurable response. A groan escaped from him. He hungrily slid his lips down her throat and chest and covered one hard little knob with his mouth. He savored the flavor of her.

Danielle grabbed his hair and arched her back, pressing her breast deeper into his mouth.

Suddenly, there was loud knock at the trailer door.

"Hey, man, you okay in there?" Butch called from the

other side of the door. "I think that quake was a five-pointer!"

Paul released Danielle's moist breast from his mouth. His breathing was heavy. His need for her was out of control. She slipped her hands free of his hair. Avoiding his eyes, she quickly picked up her top and hurried into the bathroom.

"Butch, everything's cool!" Paul called back. "I'll be out in a minute."

"Sure!"

He could hear Butch walk away from the trailer door.

Paul knocked on the bathroom door. "Danielle, are you all right?" Why couldn't he keep his hands off her? Why couldn't he just have a business relationship with her like any other architect and building contractor?

"I—I'm fine," she said in an unsteady voice. "I get scared in earthquakes, that's all."

She opened the door. Her red halter top was on. Her hair was neatly tied back in a ponytail. But she still didn't look him straight in the eyes as she walked past him out of the trailer.

Paul stood there, feeling frustrated with himself. How could he have allowed himself to caress her so intimately? With his hands and mouth, he'd told her how much he cared about her, because that's how he felt. But why was he fooling himself?

Danielle was a family woman. She needed a man who'd come home to her every night. A man who could stay close to her every day of her life. A man who'd give her children. He could never be that man.

He was a loner. He'd never be able to offer her the security and love she needed in a relationship.

That's why touching Danielle, caressing her, kissing her, hurt so bad. He knew she had no future with him. Yet how was he going to keep his distance from her emotionally and physically now that she was working in his trailer?

Inside the house, Danielle tried to concentrate on showing Butch her second-floor framing plan. Her skin was still steaming from Paul's touch. "Butch, this is exactly what I want to see built."

"Sure, Danielle," Butch replied. "No problem." Then he went back to his work.

She walked through the first floor to check each room against her revised plans, but she saw only a blur. How could she have let down her guard with Paul? What if Mr. Harrington found out she'd been in the construction trailer with her bare breast in Paul's mouth?

*Great architectural work, Danielle,* she scolded herself. *Mr. Harrington would've fired you on the spot!*

Just then, she felt the familiar gentle touch of Paul's hand on her shoulder.

"Don't get down on yourself, Danielle," Paul whispered.

It was almost as if he could see right into her.

"What happened in the trailer was my fault, not yours."

It was the tenderness in his voice, the caring, that softened her inside. That is—until her eye caught something in the first-floor framing of the house.

"I can't believe this!" she burst out. "You ruined my kitchen!"

"What?" He stared at the wooden structure.

She hurried past the worker who was hammering beams. With her hand, she slapped the half wall separating the cooking section from the eat-in area. "What's this?"

Paul looked confused. "A wall."

"No wall is supposed to be here."

"Sure it is," Paul insisted as he grabbed his set of framing plans, which were lying on a makeshift table. He pointed out the walled-in area. "Right here. You drew it yourself."

"I changed it," she retorted. She quickly showed him her revised copy. "The kitchen and eat-in area are now one big, open space."

Paul leaned over her to peer at the blueprints. "Let me see that."

She felt his body heat. His tanned skin was warm against hers. A yearning sensation crept up her body. But she wasn't going to weaken now.

"You messed up the kitchen," she continued, "because you started framing without me!"

"Danielle, I did what I was told," he said, feeling helpless.

She waved over Butch. "Please tear down the half wall by the kitchen."

"Hey, wait a sec," Paul protested. "I give the orders around here."

She put a hand on her hip. "Not when you give the wrong ones!" She hated going against him, but she had to assert her power as the architect or she'd lose it. She turned back to Butch. "Take it down."

Paul's face reddened. "Butch, don't move a muscle until I say so!"

Butch frowned as he looked from Danielle to Paul, not knowing what to do.

Danielle grabbed a hammer from the floor. "Fine! I'll do it myself!" She started banging on the wall. She was going to design the house her way, not his!

Paul pulled a hammer from his tool belt. "Hold on, Danielle. That's my job, not yours."

"Really? Then how about leaving my architectural work to me!"

She pounded the hammer harder. From the corner of her eye, she caught Butch breaking into a grin. Maybe she looked foolish to the crew, but she was going to assert her rights from now on.

Blood rushed to Paul's face. His entire crew was staring at him. No one had ever challenged his authority on a construction site, especially a woman!

"Everybody back to work!" Paul ordered.

Then he impulsively grabbed Danielle by her bare waist

and spun her around to face him. "You'd better stop..." he began, but his voice trailed off.

Her turquoise eyes stared straight into his soul. She wasn't intimidated by him at all. She'd fight him until he was waving a white flag. And he was totally mesmerized by her fierce determination.

"Well?" she challenged, ready for battle.

"Okay, okay. I screwed up your kitchen plan," he admitted. "I'll dismantle the wall just the way you want."

She pushed the hammer into his gut. "Next time, consult *me* before you work with my blueprints." With that, she glanced at her wristwatch. "I'm going back to my office to pack the rest of my supplies for the trailer. See you in the morning."

He watched her stride decisively to her car. When she drove off, Butch slapped him on the back.

"Danielle Ford's got you on a leash, man."

Paul forcefully cracked the kitchen half wall with his hammer. "No way."

"I've never seen you let an architect talk to you that way, not even Victor Horton," Butch went on. "How come Danielle Ford has that kind of power over you?"

Paul crunched the wood into tiny pieces. "I wish I knew, Butch. I wish I knew."

Danielle was affecting his insides the way no woman ever had. And it scared him. He'd always been the ruler of his own world. But when Danielle was near him, she was the throne and kingdom all wrapped in one.

At her office, Danielle hurled her rulers and pens into boxes. She stuffed her tissues and coffee cup in, too. Her stomach was churning. Was she making a terrible mistake working so physically close to Paul? How was she going to concentrate on the honeymoon house if Paul was working in that small room with her?

Just then, her office door burst open. Lisa excitedly flew inside. She held a brochure in her hand. "I found the perfect place for my wedding reception! We're going to charter a boat in Marina Del Rey!" She stopped and looked around the office. "Where are you going with your stuff?"

"To my temporary office in the construction trailer," Danielle replied.

Lisa's eyes widened. "You're going to work in the same space as Paul Richards?"

"Why not?"

"I think it's great," Lisa said. "I knew you'd fall for him."

"I haven't," she retorted. "I need to work in the trailer so I can keep tabs on him."

"Tabs?" Lisa repeated with a mischievous smile. "I dare you to tell me you're not turned on by Paul Richards."

Danielle's cheeks burned. "Okay, I am. So what? I've met other men I'm attracted to."

"Really? Who?"

"I don't remember their names!"

"Because Paul is special," Lisa persisted. "Admit it. You're joining offices because you want to spend more time with him."

Danielle was so nervous she dropped a stack of spec sheets all over the floor. "Will you concentrate on your wedding plans and forget about me?"

"I'm right!" Lisa yelped. "You're nuts about him!"

Danielle's hands were perspiring, even though the air conditioner was finally working. "Show me that wedding brochure you brought over." She had to get her and Lisa's minds off Paul.

Lisa handed her the brochure. "All right, all right, I won't bug you about Paul."

Danielle stared at the brochure in openmouthed awe. Lisa's wedding reception would be on a yacht anchored in the moonlit bay of Marina Del Rey, with sparkling stars overhead. In the picture, round tables were covered in white lace and graced with lit candles and colorful floral centerpieces. The boat had a bar, a small bandstand and a polished hardwood-floor dancing area.

"You and Manny are going to have the most romantic wedding reception I've ever seen!" Danielle exclaimed.

Lisa's eyes glowed. "Who will you bring as a guest to my wedding?"

Danielle's heart raced. Only one man flashed in her mind. She quickly handed Lisa the brochure. "Nobody." She unplugged her computer and laser printer to move them out of the office.

Lisa deliberately darted for the door. "Ask Paul to my wedding!" Before Danielle could scold her, Lisa escaped outside.

Danielle stopped packing and plopped into a chair. Lisa knew her well. She was dying to invite Paul to be her date at Lisa's wedding. There was no other man in the cosmos she desired to share that special day except him.

But she couldn't ask Paul. She knew how easy it would be to fall crazy in love with him. He was confident, strong and sexy and had a caring heart. But she wondered if Paul could ever put her first in his life.

Obviously not. He had dared to start framing the honeymoon house without letting her know, hadn't he? His priority was his potential partnership with Mr. Harrington, not her feelings.

She stood up and began taping down the packing boxes. She flashed on Paul's bare palms covering her breasts and his lips devouring hers after the earthquake. She smiled to herself. Paul hadn't put Mr. Harrington and his work first then, had he?

The sudden ringing of her telephone cut into her sensual thoughts.

Mr. Harrington's commanding voice came over the line.

"Danielle, can we meet tomorrow at the construction site? I have something to discuss with you."

"Of course, Mr. Harrington," she immediately said. "I'll see you then."

She hung up the phone, feeling uneasy. Was he displeased with her work? She couldn't let herself think negatively. She'd meet with him and regain her momentum just as she'd planned.

She shoved her coffeemaker into the box. She needed to show Mr. Harrington that his dream house was coming to sparkling life. She'd prove to him that he could trust her abilities—so much so that he'd see she was the perfect architect for his children's library.

The salty Pacific Ocean felt cold to Paul's skin as he swam under the rising tangerine sun. He made it a habit every morning when he arrived at the construction site to jog on the sand and then take a leisurely swim before his crew arrived.

Jogging and swimming cleared his head so he could analyze the architectural plans and prepare his work schedule for the day. But not this particular morning. With every stroke through the foamy waves, Danielle Ford burst into his head.

As his arms sliced through the sea, he could still feel her fleshy, abundant breasts against his mouth in the trailer. He remembered how she'd pressed her trembling body close to his, silently saying she wanted more of him, too.

He swam harder toward the shore, demanding his erotic thoughts to fade away. He reminded himself that he could never allow himself to make love to Danielle Ford. She deserved a man who was willing to commit his entire life to her—something he was incapable of doing.

As he walked on the sandy beach, his eye caught someone standing at the top of the cliff of the honeymoon house.

He realized it was Danielle. She was watching him. Her shapely figure was surrounded by the glimmering morning sun. She looked like an angel.

His heart pounded against his ribs. He wanted to wave her down and sensually play with her on the sand. But when he remembered why she was standing up there so early in the morning, he found himself hurrying toward the trailer.

She was moving into his work space. Taking over his office. He ran up the hill to see what damage she'd done to his sense of order.

Danielle's blood surged through her veins as she watched Paul climbing up the sandy hill toward the construction site. She'd gotten so enthralled watching his powerful body slice through the Pacific Ocean that she'd forgotten to hurry back to the trailer before he spotted her.

She whirled around and rushed back, hoping he'd be a teeny-weeny bit pleased at the way she'd organized their office.

She'd just made it back to the trailer, when she heard the door open behind her. "Good morning, Paul," she said, cheerily but somewhat nervously.

He briefly took in all her boxes and paraphernalia. "I didn't expect you here this early."

She tried to act nonchalant as she put away her work things. "I wanted to get my stuff settled in before you arrived."

Paul smelled of seawater. His hair glistened with ocean droplets. Her eyes drifted down to his wet, bare chest heaving with each breath from running up the hill. Her gaze went farther down to his damp swim trunks, which hugged his very ample manhood.

She swallowed and tore her eyes away. She turned to her framing plans. "I've decided to put an oak stairwell along the staircase up to the second floor instead of a wrought-iron railing."

"Hmm...interesting," he said. "Do you mind if I take a shower while we talk?"

She didn't dare lift her eyes from her plans or he'd see her face turn crimson. "Go right ahead."

Paul went into the bathroom. "Your stairwell idea sounds great."

"Do you think Mr. Harrington might like it?"

"I bet he will."

She noticed that Paul had left the bathroom door open. She heard his wet swim trunks fall to the floor. She bit her lip, wondering if she should leave the trailer while he showered.

"Jeez, what's with this faucet?" he muttered. "I can't get the shower to go on."

She felt the urge to ask, Do you need my help? But she didn't dare, knowing how vulnerable she'd feel being in the bathroom with him.

Instead she offered, "Should I call a plumber?"

Just then, she heard the water splashing down. "Ahhh, there we go!" Paul declared.

She pictured the wet spray caressing his bulging muscles, and desperately tried to concentrate on her stairwell drawing, but she kept fantasizing her hands soaping down his nude, hard masculine body.

She cleared her throat and called out in a strained voice, "I'm meeting with Mr. Harrington this morning."

"I know," Paul responded.

Her heart sank. "You do?" Had Harrington called Paul about the meeting before talking to her? Why couldn't she have her own relationship with the man? How could she impress him with her talent as an architect if Paul was always between them?

The scent of musk soap filtered out from the bathroom. She pictured Paul lathering up his powerful arms and legs with the foam.

She heard the squeak of the shower faucets being turned off. Her eyes darted to Paul's dry shorts and shirt lying on the plaid sofa. She pictured him asking her to bring them into the bathroom, or his coming out half-naked to get his clothes.

Unable to stand the torture of her erotic imagination,

Danielle headed for the trailer door. "I've got to get something from my car!"

Paul grabbed the only towel he'd brought from his apartment. He wrapped the terry cloth around his waist and walked into the office. He hadn't meant to embarrass Danielle by taking a shower while she was in the trailer.

But, heck, he needed to let her know that her presence wasn't going to change the way he operated, even though all he could think about in the shower was her being a tormenting few yards away.

Paul slipped on his shorts and T-shirt and rubbed his hair dry with the towel. That's when he noticed that she'd put some of his paperwork that had been sitting on the worktable back into his cardboard boxes of files to make room for her computer and printer.

*Hey, she can't do that!* he mentally protested. He was about to rearrange his things into their proper disorder, when he noticed her flowered pen on the table.

He gingerly picked it up between his fingers. It smelled of her sweetness. He rubbed his thumb down the smooth surface as if he were caressing her.

*So big deal, she ruffled your feathers a little by changing your office around,* he told himself. *You can deal with it, can't you?*

Suddenly, looking through the trailer window, he did a double take. He saw that Butch was standing frustrated and helpless as Danielle, with a measuring tape, was critically checking the dimensions of the dining room—dimensions that Paul was sure had been measured perfectly.

Paul yanked open the trailer door, hurled his towel who knows where and barreled over to the trouble.

In the framed area, Danielle felt her panic rise. "Butch, the dining room is short by two feet. The dimensions on my plan are fifteen by fifteen, *not* thirteen by fifteen."

Butch scratched his head. "I measured it according to the footage Paul gave me."

"Paul was way off!" she blurted.

Exasperated, she picked up the framing plans on the makeshift table and deftly sidestepped a huge puddle of wet mud behind her.

Paul was suddenly by her side, motioning for Butch to return to his work. "What's going on, Danielle?"

She anxiously pointed to her plan. "Why didn't you follow my dimensions instead of making up your own?"

"I didn't frame the dining room according to *my* specifications," he emphasized.

She glared at him. "Oh, no? Then if not yours, whose?"

He shoved his hands in his pockets. "Mr. Harrington's."

Her stomach felt queasy. "Why didn't he mention anything to me about it?"

"Danielle, he was probably in a rush," Paul quickly explained. "He called me last night, saying he wanted to meet with the two of us, and he rambled on about enlarging his kitchen and shortening his dining room by two feet."

"He wants to meet with you, too?" Danielle asked, feeling more crushed by the minute. She thought the meeting was supposed to be only between her and Mr. Harrington.

Paul gently touched her arm. "Danielle, don't worry about it. The construction's going well. I know he's satisfied with your work."

"Sure," she said, her voice dropping.

She felt torn, wanting to trust Paul, yet knowing he had his business investment with Mr. Harrington to protect.

Filled with turmoil, Danielle blindly turned away from Paul but didn't watch her step. Her foot slipped in the mud, and she went sprawling on her back in the thick, moist soil.

Paul instantly lifted her up. "Danielle, are you hurt?" he asked, worried. "Should I call a doctor?"

"I'm fine, Paul. Really. I'm okay." But she wasn't. She

was dripping with brown gook. She fingered her shorts and top, which were soaked to her skin.

"Oh, no," she groaned, remembering. "My meeting with Mr. Harrington! What am I going to do?"

Paul grabbed her hand, leading her into the trailer. "You're going to take a shower."

"But I need dry clothes!"

"Give me your sister's number," Paul said, taking over. "I'll phone Lisa and ask her to bring over fresh duds."

"You will?" she asked, feeling grateful and well taken care of by him.

While Paul was on the phone in the trailer office, Danielle slipped into the bathroom and closed the door. *Every time I'm about to give up on Paul,* she thought, *he comes through for me.* She couldn't ignore the warmth she felt from him.

She immediately shed her gooey clothes on the bathroom floor. She could feel the mud caking on her skin. Then she stepped into the tiny shower stall, which had an overhead spray nozzle and a circular shower curtain.

She pulled the shower curtain and anxiously turned the cold- and hot-water faucets. Neither moved. She gripped them more tightly and struggled to turn on the water, but the handles were stuck.

Her skin felt crinkly and rigid from the dried mud. She knew Mr. Harrington would be coming soon. She banged on the faucets, demanding them to work.

"Danielle, what's wrong?" she heard Paul call from behind the bathroom door.

"The shower won't go on!" she yelled back, tugging at the faucets, knowing she didn't have another moment to waste.

Paul stood at the closed bathroom door, aware those faucet handles were impossible. He could hear Danielle sounding more upset by the minute. Without thinking, he opened the door and rushed into the bathroom. He shoved back the shower curtain to reach the faucets.

"I'll get the water going—" His words froze in his throat.

Paul's eyes landed on Danielle's nude body, only inches from his touch. Her bountiful ivory breasts jutted forth, begging to be fondled. Her large, brown nipples grew taut from his gaze.

His breathing halted as his eyes drifted down to the fuzzy patch between her legs.

He forced his eyes to focus on the faucets. "I—I just need to loosen the handles," he stammered, finding it difficult to concentrate. "It'll take me only a second."

"Hurry, Paul," Danielle quickly said. "Mr. Harrington will be here any minute."

He noticed her glance out the shower stall, looking for a towel. He remembered having used the only towel he'd brought to the trailer, but couldn't recall where he'd thrown it.

Paul pulled out a wrench from his tool belt. "Danielle, I need to step into the shower." He strained to keep his eyes away from her naked body. "I've got to get a better grip on the faucets."

"S-sure," she stuttered, leaning against the shower wall.

Paul squeezed into the tiny stall with her. Beads of perspiration formed on his forehead. His body temperature immediately rose to unhealthy levels. He yearned to chuck the wrench and caress her nakedness with his bare hands.

He yanked at the cold-water handle. Suddenly, a gush of icy water burst from the shower-head onto both of them.

"Turn if off!" Danielle squealed. "I'm freezing!"

He struggled with the faucet. "I'm trying! I'm trying!" But he couldn't get the cold water to turn off. The frigid water continued to spray down on them like freezing rain.

He felt Danielle trying to wiggle out of the shower, but the stall was so tiny and he was so busy trying to solve the faucet problem that she was pinned inside.

As he tried to move to the side to let her out, his bare arm brushed against her hard nipples. His body reacted.

Her turquoise eyes glazed over as she gazed up at him. Her lips parted. His breathing quickened. The wrench involuntarily slipped from his fingers and clanked to the bathroom floor.

He impulsively drew Danielle's naked body against his wet T-shirted chest. His mouth found hers. The cold spray mingled with their lips. His hands slid down her glossy back and reached her wet buttocks. He squeezed the fullness of her flesh and pressed her body against his aroused masculinity.

She groaned and gently rotated her feminine spot against him. He felt her grip the loops of his shorts, wanting to pull them down. He slipped his hands lower on her derriere until his fingers touched the moist warmth between her legs. He ached to be deep inside her.

All of a sudden, Lisa's distant voice cut into their sultry shower play.

"Danielle, I'm here with your clothes!"

Danielle released herself from his arms. Her eyes were glistening with desire. Paul desperately wanted to draw her to him again and merge his body with hers.

"I'll be right out, Lee!" Danielle called back, her eyes still locked with his.

Paul quickly picked up the wrench, then yanked at the hot-water faucet, and warm water spurted out of the nozzle.

He climbed out of the shower. She slid the curtain around her. He stood there a moment as steam filled the room, needing to say something to her but not knowing what.

He pushed back his dripping hair, took a deep breath and exited the bathroom.

Lisa's eyes widened in surprise when she saw him walk out of the bathroom drenched. She stood there holding a hanger with a dry set of Danielle's clothes.

Paul's face filled with hot blood. "Just a faucet problem. It's all taken care of now."

"I'm glad," Lisa said, holding back a smile.

Feeling guilty as hell, Paul grabbed a pair of dry shorts and immediately left the trailer.

# Five

In the shower, Danielle upped the cold water, trying to simmer down her searing body. Her nipples were still pulsating. The sensitive area between her legs yearned for more of Paul's erotic touch.

If Lisa hadn't called out, would she have made love to him? A loud yes rang through her brain. No matter what conflicts she had with Paul, when they were alone, she wanted only him.

There was a knock at the bathroom door. Lisa entered. "I brought you a bath towel, clothes and your hair dryer."

"Perfect," Danielle said, getting out of the shower and drying off her heated body.

Lisa kept her eyes on her, waiting for a juicy explanation.

"Come on, Sis, what happened between you and Paul? Tell me, did he fix your *faucet?*"

The deliberate way Lisa said "faucet" made Danielle break into a giggle. "He certainly tried!"

Lisa giggled, too, as she helped Danielle dry her hair. She got dressed, aware that Mr. Harrington was probably on his way for their meeting.

"Danielle, you should've seen how red Paul's face was when he walked out of the bathroom," Lisa said. "He has definitely got it *bad* for you!"

Danielle stared at her. "Do you really think so?"

Lisa nodded. "I bet if you ask him, Paul will come with you to my wedding."

Danielle's heart swelled. But before she could say another word, she heard Mr. Harrington outside the trailer. Her stomach went into an immediate knot.

"Good luck with your meeting," Lisa said, giving her a hug and then leaving.

Through the open window, she heard Lisa say hello to Mr. Harrington and tell him that she was in a hurry and would talk to him soon.

Danielle nervously brushed her hair and straightened her blue shorts and white blouse. She took several deep breaths for confidence. She had to show Mr. Harrington that he could depend on her just as much as he could on Paul.

Outside the trailer, Paul firmly shook Mr. Harrington's hand. "I hope you're pleased with the framing."

"Extremely so," Mr. Harrington replied. "I must say, you have definitely not disappointed me, Paul. Danielle's framing plans seem to be meeting all my needs. I have absolutely no complaints about her work."

Paul smiled, relieved. "Danielle's an excellent architect. You made the right choice keeping her on. She's bright and creative and—"

"Do you find her pleasant to work with, Paul?" Mr. Harrington cut in.

The question surprised Paul, and his face heated up. "Yeah, I do."

Mr. Harrington nodded, as though he somehow sensed

that Paul's relationship with Danielle was developing into something more than just a working one.

Danielle emerged from the trailer. Her hands were trembling. What was Paul saying to Mr. Harrington? Was he telling him about the conflicts they'd had during framing? She brushed that thought aside, remembering the closeness they'd shared in the shower.

She walked over to Mr. Harrington. "I have an assortment of brochures for you," she began. "Maybe you can choose the fixtures for your master bathroom this morning."

Mr. Harrington frowned. "Actually, Danielle, the reason I arranged this meeting is to tell you and Paul that something has happened in my life. I won't be able to spend as much time as I need to monitor the construction of my house."

Danielle's eyes nervously darted to Paul. "What do you mean?"

Mr. Harrington's eyes twinkled. "My wife is pregnant."

"That's terrific!" Danielle added, excited for him, yet uneasy about what he was leading up to.

Paul gave Mr. Harrington a warm handshake. "You're going to be a father. Congratulations!"

"I'm thrilled about having a family of my own," Harrington went on. "All couples in love should feel such joy."

"I agree," Danielle said, glancing at Paul. For a split second, she wished that she and Paul were married, that the honeymoon house was theirs and they were the couple having a baby.

"I've got one problem," Mr. Harrington added, dropping his voice. "The doctor has alerted my wife and I that she has a physical problem that may cause her to miscarry."

"I'm sorry," Danielle said, remembering Lisa's telling her how much he wanted to have a child.

"I can't lose my baby," Mr. Harrington went on. "The doctor has advised my wife to remain in bed. I want to spend every free moment I can with her. So I'd appreciate if the two of you could shop for the fixtures."

Paul suddenly looked uncomfortable. "Mr. Harrington, I'll do anything to help, but you see, I'm great with a hammer and screwdriver, not choosing tubs and sinks—"

"We can do it!" Danielle interjected, not allowing Paul to ruin her opportunity to assist Mr. Harrington. "May I meet with you periodically to get your approval on each item?" She needed to keep direct contact with him if she was going to move on the children's library.

"That won't be necessary, Danielle," Mr. Harrington said. "I'm very impressed with my house so far. Your high standards and meticulous work on the framing plans have proven that you know my taste quite well."

Danielle wanted to cry out with joy at his words. "I'm so glad you're pleased, Mr. Harrington."

She caught Paul's eyes, and he was beaming at the compliment.

"Since you and Paul seem to be working so well together," Harrington went on, "I was hoping the two of you could go to the bathroom showrooms for me and choose the fixtures from a married couple's viewpoint."

Paul nervously shifted from one leg to the other. "Mr. Harrington, I'm a single guy through and through. I don't know a thing about seeing through a married man's eyes."

"Paul will learn," Danielle hastily added, seeing that Mr. Harrington was about to change his mind. "We'll pick out the most comfortable, stylish bathroom fixtures you could ever dream of."

Mr. Harrington relaxed. "Wonderful, Danielle. I think your sister was absolutely correct about you. You're very competent and very responsive to your clients' needs."

She felt like hugging him for saying that. "Thanks, Mr. Harrington."

She walked him to his Mercedes, elated that he was

finally feeling confident about her work and was relying on her decisions.

After he drove away, Danielle excitedly turned back to Paul, wanting to plan their visit to the showroom. But Paul wasn't waiting for her.

He was up on the second floor of the house, framing with Butch. She tried to catch his eye, but he had lifted a heavy beam of lumber with his muscular arms and was keeping it steady while Butch attached a metal holder for the master bedroom wall.

Her joy faded. She knew Paul was uncomfortable about picking out bathroom fixtures, but why was he deliberately avoiding her?

She suddenly realized why. He had admitted to her in front of Mr. Harrington that he was very single and wanted to stay that way.

Deep inside, she'd hoped Paul might be the man for her. But from the message he'd sent her through his comment to Mr. Harrington, she was wrong.

Wanting to forget her disappointment, she turned away from the house and went into the trailer to bury herself in her work.

On the second floor, Paul set down the beam. His heart sank as he watched Danielle disappear into the trailer. He'd felt her disillusionment with him even from high up on the second floor.

*She knows you'll never get married,* he thought. And this realization had hurt her because of how close they were getting.

He grabbed the hammer from his tool belt and furiously began pounding nails into the beam. *All you do is bring anguish to the ones you get close to,* he told himself.

Sweat poured down the front of his T-shirt. His eyes burned. The beam blurred in front of him. Without seeing, he accidentally slammed the hammer into his thumbnail.

A sharp pain surged through his finger, but he didn't

cry out. He continued hammering, feeling that he'd deserved it.

For the next few days at work, Paul experienced an inner fatigue he'd never known. Danielle kept to herself while working in the trailer. She left him a note indicating the day and time of their visit to the showroom.

During the hours he worked in the trailer with her, he wanted to explain to her that he was incapable of a married kind of love. He wanted to tell her that he'd been a loner all his life and didn't know what being in a real family was like. Instead he kept his feelings to himself, as he always had.

The night before their appointment, Paul sat alone in his cottage in Santa Monica, eating a frozen chicken dinner. He could barely taste the food.

How could he pick out bathroom fixtures with Danielle pretending he was married to her? He had no idea what a husband said or did.

When his telephone rang, he grabbed it, wishing it were Mr. Harrington so he could make some excuse about delaying the showroom appointment. Instead a familiar voice reverberated over the line.

"Skip?"

"Lucky? Is that you?" Paul asked, feeling a rush of excitement.

There was only one person in the universe who called him "Skip." His childhood friend Lucky. Lucky had given him the nickname because he said Paul skipped out of his stepmother's house whenever he felt unwanted. And the nickname had stuck.

"Skip, where the hell have you been?" Lucky asked. "I've been searching the globe for you."

Paul chuckled. "I can't believe it's you, Lucky."

His best buddy had been good luck to him when he'd needed it most. That's why he called him "Lucky." It was Lucky's house he'd run to when his stepmother called him nothing but aggravation and trouble. It was Lucky who kept telling him that his stepmother was wrong and he wasn't a waste.

"Skip, I'm living in the Big Apple," Lucky said. "But I'm moving back to the City of Angels to get married."

"Hey, I thought you and I had a pact to remain single forever."

"When you find the woman of your dreams, plans change."

Danielle flashed in Paul's mind. "She must be an incredible person for you to marry her."

With the telephone, Paul walked to his cottage window and stared at the tall palm trees swaying in the evening breeze. Danielle was the kind of woman he could see marrying—if he were the marrying kind.

"I want you to be my best man," Lucky said.

"Definitely," Paul said. "But can you see *me* in a monkey suit?"

Lucky laughed. "Absolutely. You need to practice for when you get married!"

Paul ached to tell Lucky about Danielle, but he couldn't. "Marriage isn't for me."

"Sure it is," Lucky said. "You just need to find the right lady. She'll bring love into your life."

Is that what Danielle was doing? He was too unsure of himself to believe it.

"Gotta go, Skip," Lucky said. "I'll be in touch."

When Paul hung up, Danielle permeated his mind. If Lucky could fall in love and get married, why couldn't he?

His muscles suddenly filled with tension. How could he compare himself with Lucky? Lucky had had the warmth of family love while growing up. Paul had only felt a coldness in his heart.

There was only one time the emptiness inside him had momentarily disappeared. It was when he'd met Danielle Ford.

As Danielle sat in the passenger front seat of Paul's van on their way to the showroom, she was so conscious of him next to her that she could barely see a thing out the window.

She'd tried so hard to act professional the past few weeks in the trailer. She kept reminding herself that Paul didn't share the thoughts she had about their growing relationship.

Danielle glanced at Paul as he drove. He was so quiet, so inside himself. Why force him into acting married when he wanted no part of it?

"Paul, I know you're uncomfortable about the showroom thing," she began in a shaky voice. "Do you want me to shop for the bathroom fixtures without you?"

He turned to her with a warmth and caring in his eyes that melted her inside. Then she knew why she felt so close to him.

"No way," Paul said. "We're working together on this. Besides, I dream about the shapes and colors of toilets all the time."

She smiled, feeling more relaxed. "I bet you do." Why did he always have a way of making everything all right?

Paul parked his van in front of LaVente's Showroom in Santa Monica. He tried to psyche himself into feeling like a husband. He could hear Harrington's voice replay in his mind: "Choose the fixtures from a married couple's viewpoint...married couple...married couple..."

Paul anxiously yanked open the passenger door for Danielle. His heart cried out that he wanted to think about being married to her. But why did his tormenting emotions scream back that he was destined to be single forever?

The spacious LaVente Showroom was filled with pedestal sinks and Jacuzzi tubs in rainbow shades. As Danielle entered, she could feel Paul's tense body beside her. She nervously smiled at the thin, elderly saleswoman who spotted them.

"Are you two redoing your bathroom?" the saleswoman eagerly inquired.

Paul awkwardly replied, "Not exact—"

"We're building a honeymoon house," Danielle interjected.

"How lovely!" the woman responded. "What style fixtures do you have in mind?"

"Your most romantic, erotic line," she replied, slipping an arm through Paul's, wanting to create the ambience that Mr. Harrington had requested.

Danielle glanced up at Paul, anxiously wondering how he'd take her act, knowing how uncomfortable he felt. She was surprised to see his warm, accepting smile, as though he was really emotionally connected to her.

"Let me show you our most exquisite line for a perfectly matched couple like you," the saleslady said. "Just follow me."

When Danielle felt Paul hesitate, she quickly whispered without thinking, "Relax and pretend I'm your wife."

Paul tenderly slipped his arm around her waist and drew her closer to him. "Like this?"

"S-sure," she stammered, responding to his hard body pressed against hers.

The saleswoman led them into a private display room filled with bathtubs of round, square and heart shapes.

"I know the two of you will love this one," she said, standing in front of a cream, oval bathtub. "This is our most popular Jacuzzi tub for honeymooners. It seats two adults. One button activates the jets, and a single dial adjusts the temperature."

Danielle was very aware of Paul's hand gently holding her just below her breasts. Her skin heated up as she remembered that same hand intimately touching her nipples.

"The Jacuzzi looks perfect," Danielle managed to say. She turned to Paul. "What do you think, honey?"

Paul's eyes twinkled mischievously. "The tub seems very inviting to me."

"Don't be shy, you two," the saleswoman urged. "Climb in and test the fit. You can lie cozily side by side."

Danielle hesitated. "Oh, that's okay. I can see it pretty good from up here."

"Oh, come on, *honey*," Paul encouraged. "Before we order this model, don't you think you should give it a try?"

The gleam in his eyes made her temperature rise. He was definitely enjoying the fact that now *she* was the uncomfortable one. With Mr. Harrington's task in mind, she stepped into the deep tub, sat down and leaned back.

The saleswoman smiled. "Comfy?"

"Definitely." When Danielle looked at Paul, his gaze was on her body, as though she were lying sensually naked in the tub. She felt her breathing quicken.

"Why don't you join your wife?" the saleslady prodded.

Danielle swallowed, wanting him to sit beside her but nervously anticipating her aroused response.

"Sure, why not?" Paul said, climbing into the tub and squeezing in beside her.

She could feel the warmth of his hip against her. The more he got into his husband role, the more vulnerable she felt.

"Cuddle up, you two," the saleslady said. "Don't worry about me."

"We won't," Paul said, tenderly drawing Danielle's body to his.

He smelled of aftershave. His face was close against her hair. She could barely hear the saleswoman talking.

"When the water's on," the woman explained, "the massage jet will sweep the entire length of your backs. It'll be like having a permanent masseuse in your bathroom."

Danielle imagined the water spraying onto Paul's naked body, and the swishing water traveling between her legs. She felt a hot, tingly sensation radiate across her skin.

"Will you two excuse me?" the saleswoman said as

she was waved over to the telephone in the front display room. "Enjoy! I'll be back in a minute."

When the lady left, Paul nuzzled Danielle's hair. "Am I acting married enough for you?"

Yes! she wanted to tell him. But knowing she was supposed to be working, she asked, "Paul, do you think Mr. Harrington would like this tub in his master bathroom?"

"I don't know," Paul murmured. He pushed her hair away from her ear and nibbled on her lobe. "We'd have to take a bath in it first."

Her skin got warm. "Be serious."

"I am."

Then, in the privacy of the display room, Paul lifted her chin with his finger and met her lips with his. She felt his tongue mingle with hers. Her hand settled intimately on his muscular thigh, as though he were her husband, as though they'd been married for decades.

"I'm glad you like the tub!" the saleswoman gaily interrupted.

Danielle quickly released her lips from Paul's. She realized that her hand was still on his thigh. Her face flamed. She abruptly arose from the tub.

"Yes, we'll take it," she blurted.

"I knew it!" the saleswoman exclaimed.

Danielle was relieved when Paul waited in his van while she placed the order for the Jacuzzi tub. Her body was sizzling from his kiss. She could still feel the hard muscles of his thigh under her palm.

Why deny it? She loved thinking she was married to Paul. They fit so well together—inside and outside the tub. If only the job and Mr. Harrington didn't stand between them. If only Paul wanted to get married someday as she did. If only.

When she exited the showroom, Paul was waiting for her near his van. His eyes held hers. Was he feeling married as she was?

He opened the van door for her. "Want to grab a hot dog for lunch on the Santa Monica Pier?"

She lit up. "Sure." She had work to do, but she didn't care. She couldn't resist spending more time with him.

On the Santa Monica Pier, Paul sat on a wooden bench next to Danielle, holding a hot dog with mustard and sauerkraut. On the beach below, the ocean waves lapped against the shore. Children were laughing and forming wet sand pies.

For a split second, he fantasized that she really was his wife. That there were just the two of them, enjoying the sun, the sea and being together.

When she took a bite of her hot dog, he tenderly wiped mustard off the side of her mouth with his finger. A tropical heat filtered through his body. He felt as if they were a couple, as if she were his woman.

Just then, a yellow balloon gently bounced off Paul's shoulder and flew onto the boardwalk of the pier. A worried little boy went chasing after it. Paul immediately handed his hot dog to Danielle and ran after the balloon.

He could feel Danielle watching him as he reached over the railing to grab the balloon before it disappeared over the Pacific Ocean. He quickly handed the yellow balloon back to the relieved boy.

When Paul sat back down on the bench, Danielle moved closer to him. "You were great with that little boy."

"Kids are the best," Paul said, taking a bite of his hot dog as he watched the little fellow happily running along with his parents.

"Someday I want to have three of my own." She hesitated. "What about you, Paul?"

Paul's heart momentarily filled with sadness. He got up from the bench and leaned against the railing overlooking the sand and ocean waves of Santa Monica Beach.

"I love kids, too," he said, watching the children splashing in the waves. "But they're not for me."

She leaned on the railing beside him and in a soft voice asked, "Why not, Paul?"

He stared at the blue sea. "A kid needs a parent who'll always love him and be there for him." He didn't know how to always be there for anyone. "I don't have the right qualifications for the job."

"Yes, you do," she immediately said. "You'd make a great father. You're warm and loving and caring."

He looked at her, surprised. She was saying things about him that no woman ever had. He wanted to hold her close. He wanted to tell her he felt the same about her. But something deep inside held him back.

He anxiously glanced at his watch. "Butch probably thinks we went to a showroom in Hawaii." He took their hot dog wrappers, hurled them into a trash can and took Danielle back to the construction site.

Later in the evening as Paul drove home alone from work, instead of going straight to his cottage, he found himself turning down the street in Santa Monica where he'd lived with his stepmother. He hadn't been on that street since he'd run away.

He slowed his van past his old, gray house. For a second, he thought he saw his stepmother at the front window. His stomach tensed. He felt the urge to walk up to the door and ask her why she'd never loved him, why she'd never wanted him around.

Instead he pushed his work boot down on the gas pedal and sped away.

During the next few weeks working in the trailer, Danielle sensed how quiet and distant Paul was. She regretted ever discussing children with him. She realized that she'd scared him off.

While she ordered the kitchen fixtures and appliances for the honeymoon house, Paul immersed himself in the interior with Butch. He rarely came into the trailer.

During lunch breaks, she saw him sitting outside, eating

his sandwich with Butch. He'd ask if she wanted to join them, but she knew he was avoiding being alone with her. She blamed herself for moving too fast with him.

Luckily, her mind was kept occupied by her helping Lisa with her wedding plans. She didn't tell her sister about the distance between her and Paul. She didn't want to spoil Lisa's excitement about her wedding arrangements and her upcoming trip to New York to visit Manny.

On the evening Lisa was leaving for New York, Danielle stood with Lisa in the Los Angeles Airport terminal, waiting for her to board the plane. She handed Lisa her makeup case.

"Lee, did you pack your hair dryer?" Danielle worriedly asked. "And your toothbrush?"

"Stop fretting, Sis," Lisa said. "I checked off every item on the list you made for me. You take great care of me."

Danielle gave Lisa a warm hug. "Give Manny my love."

"I'll miss you." Lisa was just about ready to board the plane, when she looked at Danielle with secret, twinkling eyes. "By the way, you dreamed about Paul Richards last night."

Danielle felt her cheeks flame. "How do you know?" She had dreamed that she and Paul were lying in the Jacuzzi tub at the honeymoon house, making erotic love.

Lisa smiled. "You talked in your sleep."

Danielle covered her mouth with her palm. "Oh, no, what'd I say?"

"You said over and over, 'I love you, Paul. I love you.'"

Lisa's plane was ready for last-minute passenger boarding. She threw Danielle a kiss and disappeared in the boarding tube.

Danielle walked back to her car in a daze. In her dream, she'd told Paul she loved him? Why had she said those words, when she knew the truth about him?

Paul Richards wants to stay single, her inner voice painfully reminded her.

Driving on the crowded freeway back to her apartment, she turned up the volume on the car radio to block out the fact that the honeymoon house was close to being finished. The framing was done. The custom metal windows had arrived and were scheduled to be installed. The drywall and stucco were ready in the wings.

Yes, she was anxious to talk with Mr. Harrington about his children's library project. But most of all, she couldn't bear the thought of never seeing Paul again.

Unable to return to her lonely apartment, Danielle decided to drive to the construction trailer, even though it was getting late.

She wanted to work on her computer. She had started designing a sketch of the children's library. Once the honeymoon house was completed, she was going to show her ideas to Mr. Harrington. She prayed she'd get the library job, just as she promised her parents.

Standing beside Butch, Paul stared in shock and anger at the broken lock on the security gate of the honeymoon house.

The brand-new custom windows and skylights were gone. The oval cream Jacuzzi tub had been stolen.

Paul had discovered the vandalism when he'd returned for a list of finishing interior items he'd left behind. That's when he'd found the house ransacked. He'd called Butch to rush right over.

Butch banged his fist on a wooden beam in frustration. "Jeez, man, they took our table saws, air hammers and air compressor. How're we gonna continue working?"

Paul felt ill. "I don't know." He'd promised Mr. Harrington he'd get the honeymoon house done on schedule. How the hell was he going to come through now?

In the dark evening, the sound of a vehicle driving into the dirt parking lot made Paul's stomach tighten into a knot. He'd called Mr. Harrington the moment he'd discovered what had happened.

As Mr. Harrington got out of his black Mercedes, Butch nudged Paul. "See you in the morning, man."

Paul nodded as Butch put on his helmet.

Mr. Harrington's face was filled with tension. "Tell me the damage, Paul."

Paul handed him a list he'd written out of all the stolen items. "My insurance will cover everything," he promised.

As Mr. Harrington unhappily surveyed the list, Paul spotted Danielle arriving in her car. He watched her talk to Butch before the construction supervisor roared off on his motorcycle.

Her eyes, filled with concern, caught Paul's. He felt his frustrations ease a little knowing she was there with him.

As Danielle hurried over to Paul and Mr. Harrington, she felt the panic rise. Without thinking, she impulsively slid her hand into Paul's. He squeezed her palm tightly for comfort.

The drawn look on Mr. Harrington's face made her feel light-headed and her legs unsteady. "Mr. Harrington, please don't worry," she told him. "I know the window manufacturer. I'll get the windows reordered and shipped here in two days. We'll install a new Jacuzzi tub right away."

Mr. Harrington shook his head. "No, Danielle," he said in a strained voice. "I want to postpone the completion of my house."

Danielle's mouth dropped open in shock. She saw her dreams crumbling before her eyes. Mr. Harrington would never see her worth as an architect. She'd never get hired for his children's library. And her heart was heavy knowing that if he closed down the construction site she might never see Paul again.

"Mr. Harrington, you can't give up," she blurted. "You put in so much time and effort."

Mr. Harrington's face looked drawn and tired. "I don't have any energy left to deal with this right now. I just purchased land for an important community project I'm working on. And my wife is having difficulty with her pregnancy." He sighed as if the universe were lying heavily on his back. "I'll have to finish my honeymoon house at a later date."

Danielle's panicky eyes darted to Paul for support. He had to help her. She knew the land in question was for his children's library. She wanted to scream out, *You can't halt construction on the honeymoon house, not now, not when I'm so close to getting the job I want more than anything!*

"Mr. Harrington," Paul began, "when you stop a construction project, the job almost never gets completed."

"I know, Paul," Mr. Harrington said in a sad voice. "But I can't spend twenty-four hours a day worrying about the next problem that may arise."

"You won't have to, Mr. Harrington." Danielle's heart was racing. She wasn't going to lose this opportunity. "I'll live in the trailer twenty-four hours a day until the job is complete."

"What?" Paul said.

"There's a bedroom and telephone," she said hurriedly. "If any problem occurs, I can take immediate action." Her blood was surging through her veins at record speed. "Mr. Harrington, I love this project. I promise—there won't be any more delays. I guarantee it'll be completed on schedule without your having to deal with a thing."

"Danielle, I'm not sure about this." Mr. Harrington hesitated, glancing at Paul.

Paul frowned. "You can't stay in the trailer alone."

She couldn't let Paul interfere. He had his partnership with Mr. Harrington. She had nothing if the honeymoon house went down. "Please trust me, Mr. Harrington. I can do it."

Mr. Harrington stared at the incomplete house with emotion-filled eyes. She knew he loved that house, too.

Just as she was about to push him further, Paul quickly said, "I'll stay in the trailer with Danielle."

Danielle's breathing momentarily stopped. Live with Paul in the trailer? Her mind was reeling. Her emotions went into a turmoil.

She was feeling confused and desperate. Her eyes locked with Paul's. Was he volunteering because he was falling for her the way she was for him? Or was he only thinking about keeping his partnership with Mr. Harrington intact?

# Six

"Fascinating idea, Paul," Mr. Harrington pondered. "With the two of you on the site day and night, the house could be completed earlier than scheduled. Of course, I can't consider the situation unless Danielle feels comfortable about it."

Danielle's heart was pounding. How could she move in with Paul? Wasn't her heart already getting too attached to his? Yet if she said no, Mr. Harrington would stop construction and her children's library dream would be permanently obliterated.

"Sure, I feel fine about it," she heard herself say, knowing she couldn't risk losing the library project *and* Paul.

Mr. Harrington gripped Paul's shoulder and warmly shook Danielle's hand. "Danielle, I appreciate your putting out an extra effort for me. I never forget a favor."

Danielle's hopes rose as she shook Mr. Harrington's hand. She knew he was someone who kept his word.

Maybe, just maybe, he'd offer her the job on his library just to pay her back!

As Danielle walked to her car, Paul stood there in total shock. Live in the trailer with Danielle? As she got in her car, she glanced back at him a bit unsurely and then drove off. What had he just done?

Mr. Harrington patted Paul on the back. "Thanks for taking over for me, Paul. Now I can concentrate on my wife and get the children's library going. In fact, I called Victor Horton and told him you recommended him as the architect. Now I need to get the rest of the financing to build it."

Paul barely heard Mr. Harrington. He stared at the trailer, desperately trying to imagine sharing every day and night with Danielle. He'd lived alone since he was seventeen years old. How could he share his living space with anyone, especially Danielle?

After Mr. Harrington left in his Mercedes, Paul sat in his van. He knew Danielle had the ability to open his heart in a way no one else ever had. Being close to her stripped away his protective shield and made him vulnerable.

That's what scared him. If he spent every day and night with her she might end up melting his heart and soul. But what if she didn't need him the way he needed her? What then?

He turned on the engine. His van sputtered with uncertainty, just like his heart.

At her apartment, Danielle gripped the telephone to her ear as she stared at her open suitcase lying on the bed, containing her nightgown, shorts, skirts and tops. The items she'd need to move into the trailer with Paul.

"Lee, I think I made a terrible mistake," she said into the receiver.

"Why are you doubting your decision?" Lisa asked from New York. "You're saving your job with Mr. Harrington, aren't you? And you're so close to talking to him about the children's library.''

"I know," Danielle began, feeling confused, "but I never should have made the living-in-the-trailer offer to him. Maybe I should call Mr. Harrington and tell him that I—''

"Are you afraid you'll fall crazy in love with Paul?"

Danielle felt a lump form in her throat. "Well, yeah."

"What's so terrible about that?"

Her heart ached. "Paul's a confirmed bachelor. He's not looking for a wife."

"Can't you see what a perfect opportunity you've got?" Lisa asked. "You'll be sharing the same living space with him. Why don't you give him a preview of how glorious married life can be?"

Danielle nervously bit her thumbnail. "How? I need to get the honeymoon house finished. I need to complete my library sketch."

She pictured herself in the trailer with Paul, peeling off her clothes at night, sleeping so near him.

"You're creative! You'll make it work!" Lisa insisted.

"But what if—"

"Manny's calling me," Lisa interrupted. "I've gotta go. He loves our wedding arrangements. I can't wait to be his missus!" Lisa smacked a kiss over the line and hung up.

Danielle didn't remember putting down the phone. What if she gave everything of herself to Paul? Would he eventually turn on her the way Kevin had?

She closed her suitcase, knowing if she kept it open a second longer she'd change her mind and never set foot in that trailer again.

Saturday morning at the construction site, Paul anxiously lifted boxes of his belongings from his van to carry into the trailer.

Butch held open the trailer door for him. "Man, you really did it this time." He followed Paul in. "Living in tight quarters with Danielle Ford? You watch. She'll dictate your every move."

Paul was already racked with reservations. Butch didn't have to rub it in. "You're wrong, Butch." He set his razor, shaving cream and toothbrush on the narrow shelf above the bathroom sink. "This is pure business."

Butch grinned. "Oh, yeah? Then tell me. Does she get the bed or you?"

He walked past Butch into the tiny bedroom. "She does."

"See what I mean?" Butch said, following him. "Danielle's got you under her thumb just like she's your wife, man."

"That's ridiculous." Paul blindly stuffed his socks and underwear into the bottom drawer of the bedroom cabinet.

Butch nudged Paul over and pulled open the top drawers of the cabinet. "Look at you. These top drawers are empty, too, but you automatically leave the best for her."

Butch was making him so nervous he dropped his jockstrap on the floor. "This is a temporary situation," Paul nervously said. He hurled the jockstrap into the drawer. "When the honeymoon house is done, I return to my place and she goes to hers."

Paul heard Danielle's car drive up. He glanced out the front window to see her opening the trunk of her car. His palms grew moist. His throat was dry.

"Temporary, right," Butch repeated knowingly. "I thought I was staying in L.A. temporarily, but I've been here twenty years. See you this afternoon, man. I'll pick you up for our meeting with the drywaller and floor tiler."

"Yeah, catch you this afternoon," Paul said, barely hearing Butch leave as his attention stayed riveted to Danielle unloading her stuff from her car.

Danielle lugged two bulging suitcases and three overflowing shopping bags out of her trunk. She saw Butch exit the trailer, hop on his motorcycle and take off.

She stared at the trailer, knowing Paul was in there waiting for her. All her fears of falling in love with the man she worked with rose up in her body like a fierce typhoon. She felt the urge to throw her stuff back in the car and take off.

Paul came out. The sensitive, affectionate look in his charcoal eyes sent a warmth through her veins.

"Welcome to the honeymoon house trailer park," Paul greeted her.

His voice was deep and sexy. Hot sparks streaked through her limbs as she realized that she'd be totally alone with him the entire night.

She swallowed and grabbed her suitcases. "I'd better get this stuff inside."

"First-class service all the way." He lifted her suitcases and bags in his muscular arms and led her into the trailer.

Inside, Paul immediately set Danielle's suitcases on the bed. He was super-aware of being alone with her in the tiny bedroom.

He cleared his throat. "I'll sleep on the sofa in the office."

"No, no, you take the bed," she said, moving toward her suitcases to carry them into the office.

Butch's prediction rang in his ears. "Danielle, the bed's more comfortable for you." He reached for her suitcases before she could move them.

She grabbed her suitcases from him. "You're taller and the mattress is longer."

"The bed is yours!" he firmly insisted, taking the suitcases and settling them back on the bed.

Suddenly, one of her suitcases opened and several items fell to the floor. As he bent to pick up her clothes his fingers landed on her lavender nightgown—the flimsy, see-through job he'd seen her wearing that night on the balcony.

"S-sorry for the mess," he stammered, quickly handing her the nightgown.

"It's my fault." She glanced at the sheer fabric in her hands and then looked up at him as though remembering. "Paul, do you recall the night you came to my apartment for dinner?"

He swallowed. "Yeah."

"I know this sounds crazy," she began. "But I thought I saw your van later that evening when I was on my balcony."

His face heated up. How could he lie to her? "Actually, I parked near your apartment building, thinking... Then you walked onto the balcony."

Her eyes held his. Her voice trembled a little. "What were you thinking?"

The words came rushing out before he realized it. "About making love to you."

Her cheeks flushed. Her lips parted. "Paul, why did you move into the trailer with me?"

"Because I wanted to be with y—" He stopped. What was he saying? Why get her hoping for a relationship he could never give her? "I want to complete Mr. Harrington's honeymoon house."

He could see disappointment fill her eyes, and he felt instantly angry with himself. Why couldn't he say the right words, feel the right feelings?

"Sure, me, too," she said immediately, avoiding his eyes.

He suddenly felt that he needed to be alone. "I didn't jog this morning. I'll run while you unpack."

He nervously reached for his jogging shorts from the bottom drawer. His jockstrap caught on his finger, flew up in the air and landed right in Danielle's hand. He caught her trying not to laugh as she stretched it out and then threw it back at him. He swiftly escaped into the bathroom.

Danielle stared at the closed bathroom door, wanting to call him back. She needed to tell him that she was sorry for probing him, for getting too personal. She knew Paul was a private man. He kept his deepest emotions to himself. Why was she already making him feel uneasy about living with her?

As she anxiously put her underwear in the top drawer, she realized that he'd left the easier-to-reach drawers for her. He was trying very hard to make this experience comfortable for her. Why did she have to spoil it by interrogating him about his intimate emotions?

Paul came out of the bathroom bare chested, wearing navy jogging shorts and white running shoes. "Be back in an hour." Then he was out the door.

She stood alone in the trailer, not knowing what to do. Their first day together, and she'd already pushed him away.

She wanted to jog after him to straighten things out. But she wasn't a runner. Yet she couldn't stay in that claustrophobic trailer a second longer. She quickly shed her perspiration-soaked top and jeans and slipped on her bikini to cool down.

Outside, Danielle ran down the hill onto the white sand of Malibu Beach to wait for Paul. She'd talk to him. But she couldn't get emotionally heavy with him. And she couldn't be too trivial, either. Oh, she didn't know how to act!

Paul pushed his legs harder as he jogged on the flat sand near the shoreline. Why couldn't he tell Danielle the real reason he'd volunteered to stay in the trailer with her? Sure, he wanted to keep the possible partnership with Mr. Harrington an option, but more important, he wanted to be near her, close to her. She was like a vital life force to him.

His running shoes splashed into the rising water as he ran. He yearned to be with Danielle without holding back an inch of himself. Why couldn't he let go?

As Paul raced back toward the construction site, he spotted Danielle up ahead near the water's edge. Her bare feet lightly splashed in the shallow foam.

Paul slowed his run. He focused on her bikini-top-clad breasts bouncing with her every step. Her long, creamy legs were firm and smooth, her buttocks full and round.

He ran faster toward the water's edge to meet her. When she saw him, he thought she'd wait up for him. Instead she smiled and then headed into the ocean. A wave rose, and just as the swell crashed, she dove in.

He pulled off his running shoes and socks. Wearing his jogging shorts, he jumped into the cold sea after her.

When he surfaced, Danielle was standing a few feet away, being nudged by the waves. Her eyes were on him. Her fleshy breasts above the bikini top were wet and shiny. Her moist hair was shimmering under the sun.

As he neared her, she teasingly laughed and playfully splashed him in the face.

"Hey!" he yelled, wiping the stinging drops out of his eyes.

She giggled and splashed him again. "Scared of a little water?"

"Are you?" he asked, sending a mountain of water her way. She tried warding off the barrage, but he kept pushing the white foam against her body.

"Stop! Stop!" she called out, giggling and trying to splash him back.

Paul grabbed her hand, but she kept frolicking and throwing water in his face with her other hand. As he tried to trap her in his arms, she pushed and squealed and giggled some more.

In their playing, her string bikini top became undone. The scant fabric slipped off her body and drifted out to sea.

"My top!" she called out, still giggling.

"I'll get it!" he yelled over the crashing sound of the waves.

Paul tried to reach for her bikini top, but a wave broke over them, hurling Danielle and him underwater. As he surfaced, looking for her, she rose with strands of hair across her face. Her turquoise eyes connected to his. Her swelling, naked breasts glistened. Her brown nipples were taut.

Paul's body responded. He pulled her into his arms. As a foamy wave crashed over them, his mouth met hers. He tasted sea salt mixed with her succulent, sugary lips. He felt her trembling, wet breasts against his bare chest. He released her lips and buried his face between her bountiful mounds.

He wanted to drown in her body and spirit. He wanted to hold her forever and ever.

Suddenly, in the distance, Paul heard a voice calling out. He turned to shore and spotted Butch waving both hands to catch his attention.

Paul had forgotten about his afternoon meeting with him. He looked at Danielle. She saw Butch, too. She sank into the water, clutching her bare breasts and biting her bottom lip.

"Danielle, I'm sorry—" Paul began, wanting to shield her. "I forgot Butch was coming."

"Don't worry about me," she said.

But he was worried. "I'll get Butch out of here," he promised.

Her eyes darted to Butch waiting at the shoreline. "Hurry, Paul!"

Feeling helpless, Paul rushed to shore toward Butch, frustrated with himself for allowing his need for her to cloud his mind. He'd forgotten how vulnerable she was. He'd forgotten they were working together. He'd forgotten that she deserved a man who would emotionally give his all to her. A man he could never be.


With the waves crashing over her, Danielle waited until Paul and Butch disappeared up the hill to the honeymoon house. She covered her breasts with her hands and rushed toward the shoreline.

As her skin burned hot from Paul's touch, she felt an

exhilaration she'd never felt before. Though neither of them had exchanged words, she felt Paul open his heart to her.

When he crushed his face between her breasts and held her tight, she felt his emotional and physical need for her. Would he have made love to her if Butch hadn't come?

In her heart, she knew he would have given all of himself. And she would have, too.

As she hurried up the path to the trailer, she searched for Butch and Paul. She exhaled with relief seeing that Paul had kept his promise. His van and Butch's motorcycle were gone. She ran inside to take a quick shower before Paul returned.

The moment she was dressed, the phone rang. Lisa's voice was on the other end from New York.

"I was talking on the phone with Mr. Harrington's secretary," Lee said, almost in a whisper. "I picked her brain about the children's library."

Danielle tightened her grip on the phone. "What'd you find out?" She anxiously turned on her computer and pulled up her sketch of the children's library.

"Tomorrow morning, Mr. Harrington is meeting with two potential financial contributors to his library," Lisa said, hurrying on. "And guess who's invited along?"

Danielle's heart hammered. "Paul?"

"Mr. Harrington wants him to be the building contractor!"

"Wow!" Her pulse raced. "Has he chosen an architect yet?"

"His secretary doesn't know," Lisa replied, a bit frustrated. "She says Mr. Harrington's spending the next couple of weeks raising the rest of the funds he'll need to build the library."

Danielle felt a surge of energy. With Paul involved in the library project, she might have an even greater chance of getting the job. She knew he'd root for her, just as he'd been supporting her on the honeymoon house.

She used the mouse to click on a file. "Lee, I've only got a couple of more weeks. I've got to finish my sketch right away."

"Go to it, Sis," Lisa said. "And don't forget to pick me up at the airport tomorrow afternoon."

Danielle quickly hung up and began fine-tuning her work. She sat at her computer for the next few hours, and before she knew it, the hour had grown late. Paul still hadn't returned.

She went to the window and looked out into the dark night. She didn't see or hear Paul's van. For a second, she felt a streak of fear that maybe he wouldn't come back that night. Had she gotten too close to him? Did he feel he had to pull away from her again?

She turned off her computer, feeling too tired to work any longer. Trying not to agonize over why he hadn't returned, she slipped into the bathroom, her lavender nightgown in hand, and quietly closed the door.

As Paul parked his van at the construction site, he struggled with his feelings about spending the night with Danielle. With the motor turned off, he stared at the light coming from the trailer windows.

How could he sleep in that tiny space with her without making love to her?

All afternoon while he and Butch were getting the final subcontractors for the honeymoon house, he'd tried to get Danielle out of his mind. He'd hoped that when Mr. Harrington had beeped him to call he'd forget his tormenting emotions.

He should have been ecstatic when Harrington had asked him to come to his Century City office the next morning. He was going to meet two philanthropists who were considering funding the children's library. Paul's partnership with Mr. Harrington was unbelievably close to becoming reality.

But Paul couldn't concentrate on his upcoming meeting

with Mr. Harrington. All he was concerned about right now was how he was going to get through the night with Danielle.

He got out of his van. Maybe he should take a blanket and camp on the beach. But then he'd be too far away from her and the construction site in case there was any danger.

Paul anxiously opened the door to the trailer. He immediately caught sight of Danielle emerging from the bathroom.

Her eyes warmed when she saw him. His heart swelled as he realized she was happy he was back. His gaze drifted down to her sheer lavender nightie. The light from the bedroom sifted through the material. Her nipples hardened in response to his visual caress.

"Is everything all right, Paul?" she asked. "You were gone so long."

She was making him feel that he was home again, that he was wanted, that he was needed. "I had to finish hiring the rest of the subs for the project."

"Oh," she said, as if her mind wasn't on the construction but only on him. "Good night, Paul."

"Ah, y-yeah, sleep well," he stammered, watching as her sensual form disappeared into the bedroom and she closed the door.

Paul took a couple of deep breaths, wondering how he was going to survive the night. He stripped down to his underwear and settled his body on the cramped plaid sofa. His long legs stuck far off the end. He turned this way and that, but couldn't get comfortable.

Then he heard Danielle shift on the squeaky mattress. He visualized her sheer gown climbing up her bare legs, revealing her succulent womanhood under the sheets.

There's no way I'm going to sleep, he thought.

He got up, opened the refrigerator and took a swig of cold milk straight from the carton.

He tried to ignore the sounds coming from the bedroom,

but as he leaned against the kitchen counter, he wanted to go to her, needed to go to her.

Finally, he found himself walking over to the closed bedroom door. *If I could just hold her for a few minutes.* He reached out for the doorknob. *You can't,* he ordered himself. *She needs so much more than you can ever give her.*

Blazing with frustration, Paul walked back into the office. He stared at the lonely, uncomfortable sofa. He couldn't take another second of lying there listening to her bedroom sounds and being unable to go to her.

He opened the trailer door. The night air was cold against his half-naked body. He didn't care. He stepped outside and closed the door behind him.

Danielle sat up in bed when the trailer door closed. She was sure she'd heard Paul just outside the bedroom. Why hadn't he come in? She'd yearned for him to.

She opened her door, went into the office and looked out the window. Paul was standing alone in the darkness. She wanted to call him back inside. She wanted to invite him into her bed so she could hold and kiss him.

Instead she slipped back into the bedroom and shut the door. In bed, she stared up at the shadows on the ceiling. Why did Paul always get so close to her and then put on the brakes?

She tightened the sheet around her body. Maybe she was moving too fast for him. She had to slow down. But how? Every muscle in her body throbbed for him.

She heard Paul return to the trailer. She turned over on her stomach and pressed her face to the pillow. *Paul, I'm here for you,* she wanted to call out to him. *Why won't you come to me?*

She held the pillow as if it were Paul. She drifted to sleep thinking about his strong arms around her, his warm lips on her mouth and his massive hands caressing her bare skin.

* * *

Early the next morning, Paul quietly left the trailer. He locked the door with the key to make sure Danielle was safe inside.

He hopped in his van and drove to Mr. Harrington's office in Century City for their meeting. He hadn't gotten a moment's sleep last night, but had spent the entire evening with his eyes open, listening to Danielle's movements in her bed. Once, he thought he heard her calling out his name in her sleep.

He pushed his work boot harder on the gas pedal as he turned onto Avenue of the Stars in Century City. He needed to forget his need for her and finish the honeymoon house as he'd promised Danielle and Mr. Harrington—no matter how much living under the same roof with her tortured him.

He drove into the underground garage of the office building. His work folder filled with the potential construction costs for the children's library tucked under his arm, Paul took the elevator up to the fifteenth floor.

In the conference room, Mr. Harrington rose from his oak desk to greet him.

"Paul Richards, I want you to meet Mr. Mulhoney of Pierce Steel and Mr. Claven of the Dynaform Corporation."

Paul firmly shook hands with both philanthropists, who were decked out in suits and ties. "Pleasure to meet you."

"Gentlemen," Mr. Harrington began, "Paul will give us the finest building construction *and* guarantee a cost-effective budget on the project." He sat down at his desk. "Since you gentlemen have requested an estimate before any architectural plans are drawn up, Paul has prepared a bid based on prior library costs and also on my ideas for the library." He turned to Paul. "Do you have some numbers for us?"

"Right here, Mr. Harrington," Paul said, handing the businessmen the list of potential construction costs. "I like to overbid rather than underbid a job, so the project will always remain in the black.''

As Mr. Harrington and the philanthropists carefully looked over the numbers, Paul's mind drifted to Danielle. He wished she were with him. Why did he feel only half-there, when he'd always felt self-contained at meetings in the past?

Mr. Harrington handed the bid back to Paul. ''Excellent, Paul. Do you have Victor Horton's résumé with you?'' He turned to the financiers. ''Paul has recommended a very talented architect whom he has worked with previously. In fact, Victor Horton is also the architect Paul suggested as part of my partnership with him.''

Paul quickly opened his folder, looking for Victor Horton's résumé. He flipped through his papers but couldn't find it. He realized he'd left it in a box at the trailer.

''I'm sorry, but I didn't bring it with me,'' Paul said, frustrated with himself. He didn't want anything to stop the momentum of Mr. Harrington's enthusiasm about their partnership.

''Why not call Victor right now?'' Mr. Harrington suggested. ''We can talk to him over the speaker phone.''

''Sure,'' Paul replied.

He dialed Victor's beeper number. ''Victor should call us back any second.''

As Mr. Harrington praised Victor Horton to the two potential contributors, stressing that Victor was Paul's personal choice, Paul suddenly felt the urge to yell out to him, No! That's not the way I feel anymore!

He realized that Victor was no longer the best architect to him. Danielle Ford was. He listened as Mr. Harrington went on and on about how Victor would design exactly the library they wanted. The more Paul heard, the more he wanted to stop the man.

But how could he? Mr. Harrington expected Victor to be the library architect, and now, so did the philanthropists. If he suddenly undercut Mr. Harrington's selling points to his potential contributors, he might jeopardize the financing of the library.

A few seconds later, the telephone rang.

"Hello, Victor," Mr. Harrington said. "Glad to hear you're feeling better. As I indicated to you on my last call, Paul has endorsed you as the architect for my library. I have a couple of financiers here who want to hear some of your design ideas."

As Victor's voice came over the loudspeaker, Paul felt his stomach muscles tensing so tight that he had to get up from the chair. He stood by the window, staring out at the glass-and-steel skyscrapers of Century City, trying to deal with the tumultuous emotions rushing through him.

In the honeymoon house, Danielle sat at her computer in her bra and panties. She hadn't had the time to get fully dressed yet. First, she had to work on her computer design of the children's library in case Paul brought up his meeting with Mr. Harrington.

Paul had left the trailer that morning without saying goodbye. She scolded herself for expecting him to act as though they were a couple. She had no right to think that way, even if she fantasized about it.

She got up from the computer to get a cold glass of juice from the refrigerator, and noticed the milk container had been left open. Paul never closed anything. She smiled to herself. She felt even closer to him knowing his quirky habits.

Her eye caught Paul's shirts and shorts hanging out of a box on the floor. He was a bit messy, too. She bent down to put his clothes back in the box, when she noticed a folder with a résumé.

She pulled out the sheet, eager to see Paul's credits. She was surprised to see that Paul's name wasn't written on top. The heading read "Victor Horton—Architect—Residential and Commercial Properties."

She nervously bit her bottom lip. Did Paul have a favorite architect other than her? Or was Victor Horton the original architect, the one Mr. Harrington said had fallen ill and couldn't design his honeymoon house?

Feeling a grinding sensation in her gut, she shoved the document back in the box. She was getting jealous over another architect's résumé. But she couldn't help it. She wanted to be first to Paul in every way. She wanted him to treat her as though she was his woman.

Yet once the honeymoon house was completed, she wasn't even sure if she'd ever see Paul again.

Determined, she hurried back to her computer. She had to concentrate on her goal. She scrolled through her computerized image of the library.

The first floor had private cubicles where children could sit at high-tech computers to research projects and discover books on the library shelves that weren't available anywhere else in the world.

She excitedly paged down the screen to the second floor. She'd designed soundproof reading rooms for preschool and elementary-school children so they could talk and laugh while looking through books without disturbing anyone else.

This is for you, Mom and Dad, she silently whispered. She was so close to talking to Mr. Harrington and showing him her sketch. She could almost hear him saying she had the job!

As Danielle polished up her work, the computer image became blurry. She'd had a sleepless night and was tired. She remembered that she had to pick up Lisa from the airport later, so she set her digital watch alarm to remind her.

Yawning, she exited her program. She laid her head on the table, thinking about Paul. She couldn't wait to find out what had happened at his meeting with Mr. Harrington. But she didn't want to push him about it. She'd let him tell her about it when he was ready. She had to take it slow with him, very slow.

Her eyelids were closing. Paul would be back in an hour or so. She could almost feel his strong arms around her body. She could almost hear herself whisper to him, Paul, I care for you so much.

As Paul opened the trailer door, he felt torn. The library project was moving very quickly. Victor Horton was set as the architect. His own partnership with Mr. Harrington was practically signed.

Why wasn't he elated? He knew why. The honeymoon house would be finished soon. He was going on to the library project, but Danielle wouldn't be with him.

As he closed the trailer door behind him, he stopped. There was Danielle at her computer, asleep with her head on the table. Her raven hair was spread across her face. Her breasts overflowed from her lacy black bra. Her satiny thighs were spread a little as she sat on the chair, and he could see she was wearing matching black lace panties.

He forced his attention away from her sensual body and noticed how uncomfortable she was. He slipped his hands under her legs and lifted her into his arms.

As he carried her to the bedroom, he stared at her beautiful face and softly kissed her on the cheek.

"Paul," he heard Danielle whisper in her sleep. "Stay close to me." Her eyes were shut. Her head leaned comfortably against his shoulder, as if she felt safe and secure in his arms.

"I will," he whispered back, feeling that he wanted to take care of her for the rest of his life.

As he tenderly laid her down on the bed, Danielle's arms tightened around his neck.

"Paul—" she murmured.

Before Paul knew what was happening, she pressed her lips to his mouth. His logical mind ordered him to stop her. She was asleep. She didn't know what she was doing. But his need for her told him otherwise. She parted her lips, and his tongue mingled with hers.

When his body became instantly aroused, he gently released his lips from hers. "You have to sleep," he said, fighting his need to hold her and caress her.

"Paul," she murmured again, dreaming. "Don't pull away. I need you so much."

Danielle tightened her grip around his neck and beckoned him down onto the bed with her.

"Danielle, we can't—"

Her lips covered his. "Paul, I love you," she moaned. "I love you."

Her words of love filled his being like a potent drug. She loved him. His heart burned in his chest. He yearned to whisper those same words back to her. But something deep inside, something cold and empty, held him back.

Danielle's eyes slowly opened. She was dreaming about making love to Paul. Suddenly, she became aware of lying in bed, scantily clad in her bra and panties. Her arms were wrapped around Paul's neck. Her lips were near his mouth. Her body was sensually pressed to his.

Her mind cleared instantly. She wasn't dreaming! She quickly released her arms from around his neck.

Paul rose from the bed, looking very uncomfortable. "I—I found you asleep at the computer," he stammered. "I thought you'd be cozier on the bed."

Her cheeks flamed. Her mind went haywire. Had she tried to seduce him in her sleep?

Paul cleared his throat and edged toward the door. "I'd better check a couple of things in the house." He closed the bedroom door behind him.

She bolted up in bed, stunned by her behavior. Had she shown Paul how much she wanted him, how strongly she needed him?

*What must he think of me?* she silently worried. *Oh, no, what did I say to him in my sleep?* She remembered Lisa telling her that she'd told Paul she loved him in a dream.

Those words would scare him off for sure!

She threw on her clothes and hurried outside to find out what damage she'd done to their relationship.

# Seven

Struggling with his emotions, Paul stood in the backyard, looking out over the Pacific Ocean. The sea breeze rushed against his face as he replayed Danielle's words in his mind.

She wanted to be close to him. She needed him. She said she loved him.

His chest expanded with warmth at the knowledge. Yet anxiety filled his body. He wasn't sure if he could fulfill her emotional needs. She'd only end up disappointed loving him.

"Paul!"

He heard Danielle's voice call out from behind him.

He turned around to see her running toward him. Her hair was still mussed from their caressing in bed. Her turquoise eyes were filled with concern.

"Paul, about what happened in the trailer," she began in a shaky voice.

She looked so vulnerable. He wanted to reach out and

stroke the soft strands of her hair. "It's okay," he said. "Don't worry about it."

She hesitated. "Paul, what did I say in my sleep?"

How could he tell her that she'd said the very words that gave meaning to his life? He couldn't let her know, because she'd need a commitment from him—a commitment he didn't know how to give.

"You were just dreaming," he told her.

"Yes, of course," she said uneasily. The alarm on her digital watch buzzed. "I've got to pick up Lisa at the airport." She waited a moment, as if she needed him to say something to her. "I'll see you later."

Frustrated and angry with himself, he watched her take off in her car. Why couldn't he burst out with the words that would meld her heart to his for eternity?

He knew he couldn't sleep in the trailer with her anymore. If he let her get any closer, she'd be hurt. Because he was incapable of giving the forever kind of love she needed.

At Los Angeles Airport, Danielle hurried to the terminal to meet Lisa. The monitor flashed that Lisa's plane had already landed. Up ahead, she spotted Lisa looking for her.

"Lee!" she called out. She hugged her sister tightly. "I missed you." She was so happy to have her family back again.

"I've got a zillion things to tell you!" Lisa said as she followed Danielle out of the terminal. "Manny will be coming in a couple of weeks. I've got an appointment with the photographer. You and I need to pick out my wedding gown and your maid-of-honor dress." Lisa stopped. "It's not working out with Paul, is it?"

"Lee, I think I spoke in my sleep and Paul heard me," Danielle blurted as she got into her car.

"Did you tell him that you loved him?" Lisa asked, her eyes wide with surprise and excitement.

She stared straight ahead at the massive San Diego Freeway traffic. "I don't know. Paul won't tell me. And worse, I woke up from my nap with my arms around his neck, and I was kissing him!"

"Perfect!" Lisa squealed.

Danielle shot her a look. "How can you say that?"

"You wanted to show Paul how much fun married life can be, didn't you?"

She turned her car off the freeway exit, toward their apartment. "I'm scaring him off, Lee."

"Danielle, you love him," Lisa said reassuringly. "Don't you know that the power of love can bind a man and woman forever?"

"I want so much to believe that," Danielle said. "But when Paul pulls away, I feel I'm losing him."

"There's only one thing you can do," Lisa told her. "Grab hold of Paul's—" she laughed mischievously "—heart and don't let go!"

Danielle parked her car in front of their apartment complex, thinking about Lisa's words. The honeymoon house would be completed in a short while. If she let Paul go now, she'd lose him forever. To keep a bachelor-minded man like Paul, she'd have to work a little harder.

That night at the trailer, Paul didn't prepare the plaid sofa to sleep on. He couldn't spend another night in the trailer with Danielle or else he'd make love to her.

He went outside to his van and pulled out the tent and sleeping bag he'd picked up from his cottage that afternoon. As he jammed the posts into the ground to hold up the canvas tent, Danielle came out of the trailer.

"Paul, what're you doing?" she asked.

He concentrated on getting the tent up, knowing he'd soften in a second if he looked at her. "I thought I'd sleep out here tonight."

As she neared him, he could smell her sweet perfume. "Do I make you feel that uncomfortable?" she asked.

He stopped and gazed at her, not wanting to say anything that would hurt her. "It's not you, Danielle."

"Then why won't you sleep in the trailer like last night?"

He forcefully pulled at the canvas to hook up the tent to the posts. "It'll be better for the two of us if I sleep out here until the house is finished."

When she was quiet for a long moment, his hands felt clammy. His head throbbed. He knew he'd hurt her anyway.

"Sure, Paul," she finally whispered, and then went back into the trailer without another word.

Paul was so frustrated with himself that he kicked one of the posts. The tent fell, and he had to start all over again.

Inside the trailer, Danielle fought the feeling that she was losing Paul. She tried to respect his decision to sleep separately from her. She'd give him the space he needed. And maybe she'd have more time and energy to perfect her library sketch.

During the next couple of weeks, the honeymoon house moved rapidly to completion. And every night before going to sleep, Danielle glanced out the trailer window to see Paul's tent sitting under the stars. She had to hold herself back from going out to him. She told herself over and over that trying to seduce him into a relationship would only backfire.

Then one night, she finally finished fine-tuning her library sketch. She was ready to talk to Mr. Harrington and ask him to choose her as the architect for his new library.

Threatening dark clouds hovered in the sky as Paul got ready to go into his tent. Wind whipped against the canvas sides. A torrential rain was approaching Malibu.

He could see Danielle sitting at her computer through the trailer window. For the past few weeks, she'd left the curtain open, as though she'd wanted him to be a part of whatever she did.

He ached to be with her. He had only a few more work-days with her. Then the house would be finished, and the construction trailer would be removed from the site. And he would return to his life and she to hers.

Drops of rain began to fall. He forced himself to go inside the tent. Under the canvas, he unzipped his sleeping bag as rain pelted the tent.

Through the plastic tent window, Paul could see Danielle go into the bathroom. A few minutes later, she came out in her lavender nightgown.

Stop torturing yourself, he silently told himself. He tore himself away from the window and lay down in his sleeping bag.

Raindrops hit harder against the canvas. A damp, cold breeze sneaked into the tent. Paul felt a chill and zipped up the sleeping bag under his chin.

He thought it would get easier sleeping alone in the tent. How wrong he was. The longer he was away from Danielle, the more he wanted her, the more he needed her.

In the trailer, Danielle glanced out the rain-splattered window at Paul's drenched tent. The downpour came even harder. Why didn't he come inside the dry trailer?

She knew why. If he walked through that door, she'd invite him into her bed. But he wasn't ready to solidify their relationship.

She could hear Lisa's voice in her head: "Grab hold of his heart and don't let go." Maybe she was giving him too much space. Maybe she was letting him slip away from her. She had to go to him. She needed to show him she still cared.

Danielle searched for an umbrella, but couldn't find one. She grabbed a blanket, put it over her head and wrapped it around her nightgowned body like a poncho.

She pushed open the door against the force of the rain.

A gust of wind caught the door, slamming it against the side of the trailer. She struggled to close it behind her so the pouring rain didn't soak the floor.

As she finally forced the door closed, her grip on the blanket came loose. The wind grabbed the blanket and sailed it across the ground.

Rain poured from the sky, soaking her barely covered body. She grabbed the doorknob to go back inside for another blanket, but the door was stuck and wouldn't open. She pulled and banged as the rain penetrated her cold skin.

All of a sudden, strong warm arms circled around her.

"Get inside!" Paul said over the pounding rain.

"The door won't open!"

He yanked at the doorknob without success for several seconds, before he swooped her up in his arms. Rain dripped down his cheeks. His hair was sodden. He held her wet body protectively against his as he headed for the dry tent.

Her heart thumped. Her breathing quickened. The rain pelted down, but she could barely feel it. She was aware only of his wet lips and his charcoal eyes gazing into hers. She knew she should tell him to put her down before they entered his tent. But she couldn't. She wouldn't. She held on tightly to him as he carried her inside.

In the tent, Paul set Danielle down on the floor. Her drenched body was trembling from the cold. He knew she'd get sick if he didn't get her warm and dry.

He immediately pulled open his duffel bag to search for his dry work shirt. "You need to get out of that wet nightgown."

"I'll be okay, Paul," Danielle said. She sneezed and coughed. Her face was pale.

"You sound great," he said worriedly. "Take off your nightgown."

Shivering, she struggled to lift the hem of the garment. The saturated fabric was plastered on like a second skin.

"I can't," she whispered, her hands quivering, her lips turning purple.

As the rain pounded his tent, Paul grabbed the shoulder straps of Danielle's nightgown and tore the fabric off her body. Her brown nipples were hard from the cold. Her naked breasts heaved with each breath she took.

Using his shirt as a towel, Paul quickly dried her face, her eyes, her cheeks, her hair. He rubbed his shirt down her back, across her breasts and down her thighs and calves to warm her up.

As healthy color returned to her face, Paul's worry subsided. He suddenly became aware of her naked breasts under his palms.

He sucked in his breath. Her glazed eyes held his. Her lips parted. The shirt slipped from his hand. He squeezed her firm globes in his bare hands and kneaded her flesh.

"Danielle—" he murmured as his thumbs circled her taut nipples.

"Hold me, Paul. Hold me," she murmured back.

He pulled her naked body to his and cupped his hands over her firm buttocks. He pressed her against his hardness.

She moaned and reached for the zipper of his strained jeans. His manhood pulsated from her touch.

Paul touched her hand, feeling close to her, so close. "Danielle, are you sure?" he whispered, knowing he desperately wanted her, but not wanting ever to hurt her.

"I need you, Paul," she breathed into his ear. "Don't pull away."

Her words melted his fears, sending hot flashes up and down his spine. "I need you so much, Danielle."

He kissed her eyes, her nose, her lips. He wanted to kiss all of her, everywhere. She slowly tugged at his zipper. Her hand pressed against his masculinity, and he groaned.

She pulled down his jeans and underwear, sending them to the floor. She whisked off his shirt and touched her lips to his bare chest. Her hand massaged his vital part until he groaned, needing to be inside her.

Paul pulled her down onto the sleeping bag and set her on his lap. She straddled his waist. As he sucked on one pert nipple, he squeezed her buttocks and slid his manhood into her depths.

She arched her back and moaned as he rhythmically moved in shared pleasure with her. Her heavy breathing further intensified his arousal. Only she existed to him. Just Danielle. Beautiful Danielle.

He moved deeper inside her. She gasped and grasped his hair as her body spasmed in pleasure. He moved faster, responding to her excitement, enjoying the depth of her secret cavern, until his pleasure began to reach the peak of no return.

He gazed deeply into her turquoise eyes, watching the bliss overwhelm her. Sensation exploded through him. He felt at one with her. There was no emotional or spiritual separation between them. He yearned to stay connected with her forever.

Before he knew it, words he never thought he'd say came out in a husky whisper. "I love you, Danielle. I love you so much."

A crescendo of sensations suddenly filled his being. His body exploded inside her, and her muscles contracted around him.

As the ecstasy subsided, Paul felt a wave of peacefulness wash over him. He lay close to her and gently kissed her lips. She was a part of him. The part that was more important than himself. He nuzzled her hair. The sweet scent of her made him feel he was in paradise. He never wanted to let her go.

She squeezed him close. "Oh, Paul, I love you!"

Her words resonated through his muscles like a balm he'd thirsted for so long. His eyes clouded. He pulled her closer, feeling the warmth of her body enveloping him.

He stroked the soft, damp strands of her hair. He wanted to stay in that tent with her for eternity. He'd be totally content, totally fulfilled. He couldn't believe what he was feeling. Paul Richards. The loner. The most unattached guy in the universe. Now he felt whole with the woman he loved.

As she lay in Paul's protective arms, Danielle felt that she was in heaven. He'd said the magical words she'd been waiting for. The words that bonded them forever.

She felt his hot breath against her hair and wanted to make love to him two, three, ten times that night.

She kissed his lips. "Paul, I feel as if Mr. Harrington built his honeymoon house just so we could fall in love."

"Me, too," he whispered.

She hugged him tight. "I almost feel it's *our* honeymoon house."

"In a way it is," he said. "Our thoughts and hard labor are in every piece of wood." He looked into her eyes. "I don't want the house to be done yet. I never realized how much I'd love working with you."

Her mind suddenly filled with light and energy. "Maybe we can work together again."

He leaned his head in his hand and stared at her as though visually caressing every inch of her. "What do you have in mind?"

Smiling with a joy she'd never felt before, Danielle grabbed the hand of the man she loved. "Come on. I'll show you!" She was ready to share her children's library dream with him.

She pulled Paul up to his feet and they hurried naked out of the tent. The rain and wind had finally stopped.

"Hey, it's freezing out here!" Paul protested, laughing. "Warm me up!" He grabbed her around the waist and snuggled against her.

Laughing, she slipped free to get to the trailer door. "You've got to see this!" She struggled with the doorknob, dying to show Paul her sketch on the computer.

He bent over her to get to the doorknob, his manhood pressed against her buttocks. "Can I help?" he whispered in her ear.

As his masculinity hardened against her, she felt herself responding. She was tempted to return to the tent and engulf herself in his sensual lovemaking. But first she had to reveal her most precious career goal to him.

"Paul, get the door open!" she said quickly, before she weakened and made love to him all night.

Paul yanked open the door. She ran past him to her computer.

Inside the trailer, Paul reached for two shirts from his box on the floor and slipped one around Danielle's shoulders to keep her warm and one on him. He wanted to take care of her, nurture her and never let anything ever harm her.

She turned on her computer right away. "Oh, Paul, look at this! I can't wait to show you!"

"Let me see," he said excitedly, resting his hands on her shoulders as he looked at the screen. He wanted to know everything about her, every thought, every feeling.

A detailed architectural drawing appeared on the monitor. "What do you think, Paul?" She scrolled down so he could view the multilevel structure.

A feeling of dread filled his gut. "What is it?"

In a voice filled with pride, she said, "I've designed Mr. Harrington's children's library."

Paul felt as though metal knuckles had smashed into his ribs. "I—I don't understand."

Her eyes twinkled with excitement. "It's my dream, Paul," she said, rushing on. "My mother and father are gone now, but they were schoolteachers. Before they died, I promised them I'd design a children's library in their honor. When Lisa told me Mr. Harrington planned to build one, I fought to get this honeymoon house job to prove to him I was the best architect for his library!"

Paul could barely hear her words. His mind was reeling. He felt his palms grow cold on her shoulders. How could he tell her that he'd already recommended Victor Horton to Mr. Harrington for the job so he could solidify his business partnership?

"Paul," she said. "Do you think Mr. Harrington will like my sketch?"

Paul felt as if he couldn't breathe. His thoughts were in a turmoil. "Why did you wait so long to say something?" If she'd told him earlier he might have been able to dissuade Harrington from Victor Horton. But how? Mr. Harrington had had doubts about Danielle's experience initially. He would have never considered her for the children's library.

Danielle slipped her arms around his neck. "I couldn't tell you before this moment because I had to be sure about our relationship. I used to go with a guy I worked with a few years ago. He put his career goals ahead of us as a couple." She leaned her head on his shoulder. "But I trust you with all my heart, Paul."

Paul felt ill. "When do you plan to show Mr. Harrington?"

"The second I get a chance to see him."

As Danielle exited her computer program, Paul stared out the trailer window. He could barely see the honeymoon house in the darkness. How was he going to break the horrible news to her that she had no chance of getting the library project because he'd handed it to another architect to better his own business?

Danielle grabbed his hand and pulled him to bed with her. She shed both their shirts and snuggled next to him naked under the sheets.

She kissed him on the mouth. "I love you so much, Paul," she whispered.

Paul should have told her right then and there to forget her dream of designing a children's library because he'd gotten Victor Horton the job. But her words of love echoed in his mind. He'd found the love he'd been yearning for all his life. Couldn't he treasure her love for just a little while longer?

As she slid her body on top of his and made love to him, all thoughts of the library and Victor Horton faded from his mind. All he was conscious of was the warmth and closeness he shared with her—a love he'd never felt before.

Afterward he lay on his back, awake. He listened to Danielle's soft breathing as she slept with her head on his chest. He tenderly stroked her hair. He realized how precious she was to him. He didn't want to lose her. But once she found out he hadn't recommended her to Mr. Harrington, would she turn away from him?

He watched the rising orange sun through the trailer window. He tried to figure out what he was going to do. The library deal was locked, wasn't it? His partnership with Mr. Harrington depended on having Victor Horton as the architect.

He couldn't lie in bed anymore. He gently released himself from her arms, threw on some clothes and left the trailer, wondering what the hell he was going to do.

Danielle awakened, sensing that Paul had left their bed. "Paul?" she called.

She got up, grabbed his work shirt and opened the trailer door. The brisk morning air hit her face. She smelled the salty sea. The honeymoon house lay still and quiet. And Paul's van was gone.

Goose bumps prickled her skin from the cool sea air. Seagulls flew above her. She could barely hear the waves flapping to shore below the cliff.

She wrapped her arms across her chest. She'd sensed something was wrong last night after showing Paul the sketches of her children's library. Did he think she was pressuring him to talk to Mr. Harrington about getting her the job?

She wished he were with her so she could tell him how much she loved him and how she'd never let work get between them.

She glanced at her watch. She planned to meet Lisa in a couple of hours to shop for Lisa's wedding gown and her own maid-of-honor dress. But first, she had to do one thing.

She put a copy of her computer design of the children's library onto a disk and slipped the disk into her bag. She had no more time to waste. She was going to show Mr. Harrington her design.

Before Danielle left the trailer to meet Lisa, she cut out a paper heart for Paul. Inside, she wrote: "Paul, no matter what, I'll always be here for you." She left the heart on the table for him, hoping he'd feel the warm love that was burning in her heart.

In Century City, Paul waited in the reception area of Mr. Harrington's office as the secretary went to announce him. He nervously flipped through a magazine without reading a word and put it back down on the coffee table.

He mentally rehearsed what he planned to say to Mr. Harrington. He'd tell him that Victor was an excellent architect, but Danielle was better. He'd talk him into looking at Danielle's computer sketch of the library. Once Mr. Harrington saw the brilliance of her work, Paul was sure Harrington would want her to design his library instead of Victor.

"Paul, perfect timing," Mr. Harrington said as he came out of his office and motioned Paul inside. "The city planning commissioner just left. He was very pleased with Victor Horton's rough drawings."

"Victor got his plans to you already?" Paul sputtered.

"He most definitely did—and quite speedily, I must add," he replied.

Paul's stomach muscles tightened. He watched tensely as Mr. Harrington leaned over Victor's blueprints on his desk.

"Paul, the city's only problem with Victor's design is the parking," Mr. Harrington began. "I must get the situation resolved quickly. I don't want a conflict with the city."

Paul's mind was reeling. How should he approach Mr. Harrington about Danielle's design? "What's wrong with Victor's idea, Mr. Harrington?"

"Victor's design has an underground parking structure," Harrington went on. "I don't feel comfortable with small children going underground to get to my library. However, the city doesn't want the library's patrons to park on the neighborhood streets. For Victor's plans to be approved by the city, the parking issue must be settled." He handed Paul a paper with notes. "Could you give this list to Victor so he can change his plans according to my specifications?"

Before Paul could answer, Mr. Harrington's secretary buzzed him that his wife was on the phone. Mr. Harrington immediately looked worried and picked up the call. Then he glanced at Paul.

"By the way, I forgot to ask why you surprised me with a visit."

Seeing how concerned Mr. Harrington was about his wife, Paul immediately said, "We'll talk another time, Mr. Harrington."

In the underground parking lot, Paul climbed into his van and stared at Mr. Harrington's note for Victor. He wanted to crumple it up and hurl it out the window. Instead he slipped the paper into his shirt pocket. He couldn't take out his frustration on Mr. Harrington or Victor.

He had to resolve the situation himself. But how? Victor's design was already with the city planning commission. How could he recommend Danielle's sketch to Mr. Harrington and the financial contributors at this phase of the project?

Yet he desperately needed Danielle in his life and couldn't risk losing her love by telling her that *he* was the reason her library dream wouldn't come true.

As he sat in his van, he felt as if his limbs were being torn from his body. He had to find a resolution somehow. He had to hold on to his love for Danielle.

# Eight

In the bridal shop, Danielle excitedly waited for Lisa to try on a white gown in the dressing room. "Lee, do you need any help?"

"Danielle, wait till you see how I look!"

She nervously glanced at her watch. She'd already told Lisa that in an hour or so she was going to Mr. Harrington's office to hand him her computer disk with her children's library sketch. She was readier than ready.

Lisa walked out wearing a snowy white, lacy, A-line gown with a vee-neck and down-to-the-wrist lace sleeves.

Danielle's breath caught in her throat. "Lee, you look gorgeous!"

Lisa's eyes glowed. "I love the gown, too!"

Without realizing it, Danielle glanced at her watch again, and Lisa didn't miss it.

"Danielle, you can't just walk into Mr. Harrington's office and ask him for the library job."

"I can't wait anymore," Danielle stated. "Besides,

when he sees my sketch, he'll want to hire me. I just know it."

Lisa appeared worried. "Are you sure he hasn't chosen an architect already?"

"Paul would've told me," she insisted. "I told him how much this job means to me."

"You really trust Paul, don't you?" Lisa asked.

"Completely."

Lisa smiled. "That's great! You can *finally* work in harmony with the man you love."

Danielle glowed with confidence. "I'm so happy, Lee! I've got a man who respects my career goals as much as I respect his."

"So?" Lisa peered at her angel-white reflection in the dressing room mirror. "Will Paul be your guest at my wedding?"

Danielle felt a jolt of nervousness and excitement. "I don't know if he'll want to go with me."

Lisa was surprised. "You haven't invited him?"

In a sheepish voice, Danielle replied, "Not yet."

"Get on it, Sis!"

Danielle held up a flowing, royal-blue lace gown against her body and looked in the mirror. She wondered if Paul would like it.

"Paul will love it!" Lisa said, reading her mind.

"You think so?" She quickly removed her clothes and slipped on the gown.

The royal blue made her eyes stand out. The see-through lace revealed her cleavage.

"Paul will propose to you the minute he sees you," Lisa went on.

"Propose?" Danielle repeated, hearing the word echo in her mind a zillion times. Would Paul ever ask her to marry him?

She stared in the mirror at her royal-blue reflection. She pictured Paul at her side in a black tuxedo, his hand possessively around her waist. She ached for that vision to come true.

Lisa nudged her. "Come on! Let's buy my wedding gown and your blue dress!"

Danielle cautiously took off the flowing lace, excited about Lisa's wedding, inviting Paul, and going directly to Mr. Harrington's office to present her sketch.

Inside the honeymoon house, Paul installed the brushed-chrome doorknobs on each interior door on the first floor, while Butch took care of the second-floor hardware.

Paul kept glancing out the front window, looking for Danielle. He reached into his pocket for a screw and found Mr. Harrington's note with the parking requirements. When he had called Victor Horton about the instructions, he'd felt like a traitor to Danielle. Yet what other choice had he had? He'd promised Mr. Harrington he'd get Victor the changes. He couldn't break his word.

Just seeing the note in his hand made him so angry at himself that he had to stop working. He crumpled the paper into a ball, wishing he'd never mentioned Victor Horton's name to Mr. Harrington.

Taking a break, Paul went into the trailer, still holding the crumpled note. He saw Danielle's paper heart lying on the table and gingerly picked it up. Her words sang out to him: "I'll always be here for you."

He swallowed hard as he tenderly held her paper heart between his fingertips. He never thought he'd have a lasting love. But with Danielle, it seemed so possible. With her, he felt he could stop running. He felt they shared a love that might last forever.

But his heart wrenched. He'd finally found love, but he was so afraid of losing it.

In Mr. Harrington's office, Danielle anxiously entered the reception area, holding her computer disk tightly. Mr.

Harrington's secretary was on the telephone.

Danielle remembered her first visit to the Century City office. She'd desperately wanted to design the honeymoon house. And she'd gotten that job. Maybe, just maybe, she'd get the children's library project, as well!

The moment the secretary hung up, Danielle took a deep breath of courage, introduced herself and said, "I don't have an appointment, but I was hoping I could see Mr. Harrington for a few moments."

Before the secretary could respond, the phone rang again. The secretary smiled apologetically and answered it.

Danielle stared at the closed door to Mr. Harrington's private office. She wanted to barge in and present her design. She wanted him to get so excited he'd hire her that very moment!

"Ms. Ford," the secretary began as she hung up, "I'm sorry, but Mr. Harrington isn't in his office. His wife went into premature labor, and he rushed her to the hospital."

"Is Mrs. Harrington okay?" Danielle asked, forgetting her plan. "Did she have the baby?"

"Not yet," the secretary replied. "When Mr. Harrington calls in, I'll be sure to tell him that you stopped by."

"Don't bother," she quickly said. "I'll talk to him when he's got less on his mind."

Danielle left the office worried about Mr. Harrington, his wife and baby. She put her computer disk back in her bag, disappointed that she'd have to keep her dream on hold a little longer.

In the hardware store, Paul felt anxious as he bought bulbs for the recessed lighting in the honeymoon house's master bedroom. Before he'd left the trailer, he'd gotten a call from Mr. Harrington. His wife was in painful premature labor. Mr. Harrington prayed that he wasn't going to lose his baby or that anything might happen to his wife.

Before Paul could express his concern, Mr. Harrington broke the news. He said that Danielle's work on the house was completed. And since there was only minute finish work to do and the security system had already been installed, he wanted the construction trailer removed from the site in the morning.

Paul paid for the bulbs feeling numb inside. He couldn't believe it. This evening would be his last with Danielle in the trailer.

In the parking lot, he shoved the bulbs onto the passenger seat of his van and started driving. How could he go on to the library project without Danielle? He'd gotten so used to living with her that he almost felt they were married.

Married. The word both frightened and excited him. He never thought he'd consider marriage for himself. Yet with Danielle, he felt that his very being had merged with hers. He couldn't be without her.

But Danielle's dream of the children's library plagued him. He couldn't tell her. Not yet. Not until Mr. Harrington's wife and baby were okay and he could talk to him about Danielle.

In the midst of his errands, he stopped at a liquor store and bought a bottle of wine. He wanted his last evening at the honeymoon house with Danielle to be very special. He wanted to show her how much he loved and needed her.

At the trailer, Danielle carried in a grocery bag filled with pasta, mozzarella and ricotta cheese, Italian bread, tomatoes and spices. She wanted to cook an Italian meal for Paul so she could cheer herself up. Once in his arms, she'd forget her anxiety about the library project and blend her soul with his.

She put the bags on the kitchen counter, wondering where Paul was. If he was going to be back late, would he call her? She laughed at herself. She was acting as though she was his wife.

She wondered if she should share her disappointment about going to see Mr. Harrington with Paul. She decided not to. She didn't want to put an ounce of pressure on him. She wanted to keep her career goals separate from their special love.

As she set down the computer disk with her library sketch, she saw a crinkled note on the table in Mr. Harrington's handwriting.

She picked it up, realizing that Paul must have left it there. In the note, Mr. Harrington had outlined specific parking needs for his children's library.

Her heart raced. Did Paul purposely leave the note for her to see? Was he trying to help her get the library job? She wanted to cheer out loud with excitement. Maybe Paul had left Mr. Harrington's instructions so she'd be that much closer to pleasing Mr. Harrington.

She wanted to hug and kiss Paul for supporting her dream. But since he'd carefully placed the note so she could find it, rather than telling her himself, she figured it would be best not to mention a thing to him until after she got the job.

She hurried to her computer, wanting to give Mr. Harrington exactly the parking structure he needed. On the screen, she narrowed the circumference of her two-story building and made the library three stories high to maintain the book space.

With the additional space, she drew an ample-sized outdoor parking lot alongside the library building. To please the city, she added parking meters to add revenue to the city's crunched budget.

"Done!" she said excitedly. She made two computer disks of her library design. She put one into her bag to show Mr. Harrington and left one near her computer as a backup.

With a jolt of enthusiasm and an overwhelming feeling

of love for Paul, she started chopping garlic for her scrumptious tomato sauce. She had to hurry so she could get dressed for her special dinner for him.

She had definitely made up her mind. She was going to ask Paul to Lisa's wedding tonight!

The moment Paul walked into the trailer, he heard soft music on the radio. He smelled delicious tomato sauce in the air. He felt he was home.

His breath was knocked away when he saw Danielle. She was leaning over, putting a pan into the oven. Her silken hair was swirled up on her head and held by a shiny gold comb. Her ivory shoulders were bare except for the black spaghetti straps of the formfitting dress she wore.

The black fabric of the dress hugged her rounded buttocks. He swallowed when he realized she wasn't wearing any panties.

Danielle turned around. "Paul!" she greeted him excitedly, as though he was the most important person in the universe.

Her breasts bounced freely under the flimsy chiffon as she came to him. She kissed him on the lips. The taste of rose perfume touched his mouth.

"Paul, I hope you're hungry because—" She stopped. "What's wrong, Paul?"

His stomach churned. "Mr. Harrington is removing the trailer tomorrow."

The glow in her eyes faded. "Oh, no," she whispered. "This is our last night at the honeymoon house?"

He nodded, wanting to say they'd still be together tomorrow and the day after that. But he couldn't utter the words. If he loved her, why couldn't he tell her that he'd be with her for always?

Danielle looked up at him. Her turquoise eyes were misty. "Can we wait on dinner and go into the house first?"

"Sure," he said, taking her hand, yearning to say the phrase that would keep them together forever.

Under the star-filled sky, Danielle felt scared. This was her last night at the honeymoon house. Her last night living with Paul. It couldn't all end. Not when she felt so close to him.

Paul disarmed the security system and opened the front door. He flipped on the recessed lights in the living room.

"I love this house," she whispered. She slipped her arm through Paul's and rested her head against his broad shoulder.

In the past few months, she'd looked at the house through the critical eyes of an architect, making sure there were no flaws. Now she was gazing at it through the eyes of a woman unbelievably in love.

The living room hardwood floors sparkled. The fireplace was white, modern with opaque glass doors. The room glistened with warmth and coziness.

"Paul, let's pretend this is our honeymoon house," she said. "Just for tonight."

Paul swooped her up in his arms. "Like this?" He brought her back outside into the darkness. Then he carried her over the threshold like a groom with his bride.

Danielle felt a burst of joy. "I feel like we're marr—" She stopped herself and quickly added, "*Mar*velously happy!"

She couldn't spoil the beautiful moment between them. She didn't want to scare him off. Not when he was feeling so close to her.

"Let's do it the right way," Paul whispered as he carried her up the winding staircase to the beige-carpeted master bedroom.

Inside the bedroom in Paul's arms, she held tightly to him and gazed at the floor-to-ceiling window facing the moonlit ocean. Paul's window. She couldn't stop herself from putting his design into her plan.

As Paul set her feet down on the carpeting, she fantasized that she really was in their own honeymoon house. She gently outlined his mouth with her finger. He parted his lips and sucked on her fingertip.

Her body stirred with desire. She covered his mouth with hers, knowing Paul was everything she'd ever wished for in a man. She didn't want the honeymoon house to be finished. She didn't want the trailer to be taken away. She wanted to be with Paul forever.

Paul released her silken hair from the gold comb. Then he slipped a finger under her spaghetti straps and slid them off her shoulders. His lips found the hollow of her neck. Her body tingled as his tongue tasted her skin.

He slowly unzipped the back of her dress. She felt the chiffon glide to the floor.

She stood trembling and naked in front of him. He gazed at her body as if admiring a goddess. She felt her nipples harden as he visually caressed her breasts and the feminine area between her legs.

In a husky voice, Paul murmured, "Turn around."

As Danielle obeyed, he slid his arms around her from behind and cupped her breasts with his large palms. She moaned softly as he squeezed her nipples.

He quickly shed his clothes, and his naked skin felt fiery hot as he pressed his manhood against her bare buttocks. He smoothed his hands down her belly, settling his fingers between her legs.

As he intimately explored her moist cave, she groaned and leaned back against his hardness.

She heard a deep moan escape from his lips.

"Danielle, I need you so much."

He spread her legs from behind and slipped his masculinity inside her. She gasped as her entire being filled with his presence.

Paul thrust deeper and deeper, until spasms of pleasure radiated through her body. He cupped her buttocks and spread them farther apart, sinking into the depths of her soul.

She cried out in ecstasy as she ebbed and flowed with the gyrations of his body. She felt his manhood growing to explosive proportions.

"Paul, you're everything to me," she whispered, forgetting her fears of scaring him off, needing to tell him the secrets of her heart.

In that instant, she felt Paul's body reach the pinnacle and his spirit merged with hers in ecstasy.

As her breathing slowed and the peacefulness of their lovemaking settled over her, Paul drew her close. His eyes were filled with love.

"Danielle," he murmured. "My Danielle."

As Paul gently held her body to his bare chest, she forgot that it was their last night at the honeymoon house. She forgot about the children's library. Her entire universe was Paul.

He lifted her in his arms and carried her back to the trailer. In the bedroom, he laid her on the bed and snuggled up to her under the sheets.

As he held her close, she fell asleep in his arms, dreaming of how fulfilled and happy she was. Dreaming about waking up and being with him forever.

The ringing of the telephone cut into her beautiful dreams of her and Paul together. She opened her eyes to find the morning sun filtering through the windows.

"I'll answer the phone," she whispered to Paul, who was barely waking up.

Danielle floated into the office on a heavenly cloud. Her heart was bursting with love. She knew the trailer would be removed later that day, but it didn't matter somehow. Her fantasy of being with Paul forever seemed so real.

She put the receiver to her ear and heard Mr. Harrington's tired voice.

"Danielle, please forgive me for calling so early in the morning."

Danielle held her breath, afraid to ask the question. "Mr. Harrington, are your wife and baby okay?"

There was a long moment of silence. Then, in a deeply emotional voice, Mr. Harrington replied, "I have a beautiful son. David weighs only five and a half pounds, but he's strong and a fighter."

Danielle's heart filled with delight. "A boy? Oh, Mr. Harrington, that's wonderful!"

Just then, Paul walked in. He grinned upon hearing the news and slipped his arm around her naked waist.

But as she handed him the phone and he spoke to Mr. Harrington, the tension building in Paul's voice suddenly made her feel uneasy.

"Of course, Mr. Harrington," Paul said. "We'll leave right now." He hung up with a preoccupied look on his face.

"What'd he say?" she asked, concerned.

"Tomorrow morning, Mr. Harrington's taking his wife and son up to San Francisco, where his wife's family lives," he replied. "He wants us to come to the hospital so he can go over the last-minute details about the honeymoon house."

As Danielle got ready to go, her mind was reeling. This was it. Was Paul going to mention a future with her? He hadn't said a word to her since Mr. Harrington's call. Why was he so quiet? Was he regretting last night?

While Paul waited for her in his van, she quickly printed out a copy of her library sketch and slipped the printout into her bag.

As she hurried into Paul's van, she not only worried about her future with Paul, but she was nervous about seeing Mr. Harrington. She was determined to show him her library drawing before he left for San Francisco.

In the hospital corridor, Paul held tightly to Danielle's hand. He felt that they were truly a couple, that he'd been with her for eons. He wasn't going to let anything interfere with the special love he shared with her.

Especially the children's library. He was going to get Mr. Harrington alone and tell him about Danielle's sketch. He was going to let him know that Danielle was the best architect he could hire for the job, not Victor Horton.

Danielle tugged at his hand. "Paul, look! There's the nursery!"

She led him to the glassed-in room filled with bassinets. He peered at all the precious newborn babies wailing and sleeping.

"What cute babies," Paul heard himself say, squeezing Danielle's hand.

"There's Mr. Harrington's baby boy!" she said, pointing to a peaceful sleeping tot with the name David Harrington written on the bassinet. "Paul, he's adorable. He's got Mr. Harrington's long nose."

Paul's heart welled with emotion at the miracle of Mr. Harrington's son lying in the bassinet. For a second, he pictured Danielle's and his baby lying there looking beautiful like her.

Just then, Mr. Harrington walked over to them. "What do you think of my son?" he asked with pride, handing Paul a cigar.

Paul swallowed the lump in his throat. "You're a lucky man, sir."

"How is your wife?" Danielle asked.

"My wife is feeling wonderful," Mr. Harrington replied, totally relieved. "She's asleep right now, so I have time to complete my business with the two of you."

Paul anxiously followed Danielle and Mr. Harrington down the hospital corridor, his muscles aching with tension. He had to get Mr. Harrington alone so he could discuss Danielle with him.

In the waiting room, Danielle sat beside Paul on the sofa across from Mr. Harrington. She clutched her bag. Inside was the computer printout of her sketch of the children's library. It wasn't three-dimensional like her sketch on the computer monitor, but she had to act fast, before he left for San Francisco.

Mr. Harrington handed Danielle her final payment. "Danielle, I must commend you on your brilliant architectural work on my honeymoon house."

Danielle's cheeks warmed. She felt Paul lightly touch her hand, silently saying he felt that way, too.

"I'm so happy you're pleased, Mr. Harrington." She nervously clasped and unclasped her hands in her lap. *Wait a few more minutes,* she told herself. *The right moment will spring out at you.*

"Paul," Mr. Harrington began, "while I'm in San Francisco, could you arrange for the movers to get our furniture and belongings into the house?"

"I'll call a moving company today," Paul replied.

"Fantastic," Mr. Harrington said. "By the way, Paul, I'd like to have a few minutes with you."

Danielle felt her heart drop. She anxiously stood up, gripping her bag. Had she lost the special moment she was waiting for? No, she wasn't going to think negatively.

She noticed Paul quickly get up and go to the water dispenser. He seemed nervous about something as he downed a cup of water and then filled up another cup.

She couldn't leave. She was afraid she'd miss her opportunity. She took a deep breath of courage. "Mr. Harrington, there's something I'd like to ask you."

"Of course, Danielle," Mr. Harrington said. "What is it?"

She swallowed. "I was hoping you might consider me as the architect for your—"

Paul suddenly started choking on the water. He hurled the paper cup into the trash and grabbed her hand. "Would you excuse us, Mr. Harrington?" He rushed her out of the waiting room.

In the hospital corridor, Paul's heart was pounding. He

barely saw the nurse who walked past, or the man carrying a bouquet of flowers into a hospital room. He couldn't concentrate on anything around him except Danielle.

Danielle stared at him. "Paul, why did you do that?"

He nervously bit the inside of his mouth. "I need to talk to you."

"Can't it wait?" she asked. "I've got to talk to Mr. Harrington before he leaves for San Francisco."

He took both her hands in his, not wanting to hurt her. "Let me have a few seconds with him first."

She reluctantly nodded. "Okay, I'll wait."

He wished he could tell her that he was going to prepare the road for her. But he couldn't promise her anything until he was sure himself.

"I'll call you in a few minutes," he said, hurrying back into the waiting room and making sure to close the door behind him.

Danielle walked to the nursery window, feeling confused. Why was Paul acting so strangely? She got the distinct impression that he'd deliberately pulled her away from Mr. Harrington so she couldn't talk to him. But why?

She peered with awe at tiny David Harrington. His little mouth opened wide in a huge yawn.

She sensed that Mr. Harrington wanted to discuss the children's library with Paul. Was Paul trying to keep her out of the project? She brushed that thought aside. Paul would never do that. He loved her.

Just then, she felt a finger tap her on the shoulder. She turned around to find a tall thin man wearing tan jeans and a plaid shirt standing near her.

"Excuse me," the man began, "I'm looking for the waiting room." His face turned crimson. "I'm not here to visit my wife or anything. I'm supposed to meet someone on business."

Danielle's gaze froze on the rolled-up architectural blueprints under his arm. A dull ache drifted through her bones.

"Are you looking for Harwood Harrington?" she asked in a strained voice.

"Why, yes, I am," he replied. "Are you acquainted with him?"

She nodded, unable to speak.

He extended his hand. "I'm Victor Horton."

Danielle's throat went dry. Her lips felt parched. Victor Horton? Then she recalled Victor Horton's résumé in Paul's box at the trailer.

"So you're Danielle Ford," Victor said with admiration. "I'm looking forward to seeing the honeymoon house you designed for Mr. Harrington. Actually, I was hired as the architect on the house, but I ended up at home for three months with mononucleosis. However, I plan to stay very healthy for his new project."

Danielle felt the blood drain from her face. "What building will you be designing for him?"

"Actually, I should be hush-hush about it," Victor went on. "You see, Paul is trying to finalize a business partnership with Mr. Harrington whereby I'm the architect on all their future projects." Victor shifted the blueprints under his arm. "Paul pushed to get me hired as the architect on this new project so he could cement his deal with Mr. Harrington."

"I—I see," she stammered. The hallway seemed to be spinning around her. It couldn't be happening to her again. Paul couldn't be a traitor to her like Kevin. Not Paul!

Just then, Victor turned away from her and looked at someone down the hallway. "Hey, Paul! I solved the library parking dilemma you called me about."

In a whirl of emotion, Danielle stared at Paul as he approached them. His face was ashen. Victor said a few words to him. But Danielle couldn't hear. She didn't want to listen. She remembered the notes she'd found in the trailer. Paul hadn't left them for her. He'd never intended to help her. He was only concerned about himself.

She didn't notice Victor walking toward the waiting

room to meet with Mr. Harrington. She barely heard Paul say something to her.

She heard the cries of newborn babies as she rushed toward the elevator. With a trembling hand, she pushed the down button, demanding the elevator to come so she could get away, far, far away, from Paul Richards.

"Danielle!"

She heard Paul call out from behind her, but she didn't turn around. She kept pressing that button and staring at the up and down arrows above the elevator. Please hurry! she silently screamed at the elevator.

Paul stood beside her, out of breath, his voice straining. "Danielle, I was going to tell you about Victor, but—"

She whirled around and glared at him. "But you didn't want to ruin your precious partnership with Mr. Harrington, did you?"

"Danielle, let me explain—"

"Don't bother." When Paul reached out to touch her, she pulled away. "Just leave me alone."

The elevator doors opened. She squeezed in with the other passengers. She didn't look at Paul. She didn't dare. As the doors closed, she fought the tears burning in her eyes.

In the lobby, she rushed out of the elevator. She remembered she'd come to the hospital with Paul, and her car was still at the honeymoon house.

She went to a public phone. Instead of calling a cab, she found herself dialing Lisa's work number. She needed to hear her sister's voice.

How could she have trusted Paul to be like family to her? How could she have fooled herself into believing that working together with him wouldn't interfere with their relationship?

Now her dream of the children's library was shattered. And Paul Richards—the man she loved—had backstabbed her to further his own career.

"Danielle, what's the matter?" Lisa asked worriedly over the phone.

The moment she heard her sister's concerned voice, her defenses crumbled. As the tears flowed down her cheeks, she heard herself reply: "Paul's not coming to your wedding."

In the maternity waiting room, Paul stared out the window as Mr. Harrington and Victor looked over Victor's parking structure plans. In his mind, all he could see was Danielle's stricken face as the elevator doors slammed between them.

He momentarily closed his eyes, trying to block out the horror of what he'd done. He clenched his fists so hard that his knuckles throbbed with pain. But he didn't care. Danielle was hurting, and it was all his fault.

"Paul, can you take a look at Victor's new design," Mr. Harrington requested. "I think it might be a bit menacing for tykes entering the building."

Paul forced himself to look at the blueprints. The parking structure was situated on the first floor of the library instead of underground. The columns and floors were concrete. Above the first-floor parking were the second and third floors with the books.

Everything in Paul wanted to scream out that all that mattered to him was Danielle, not the library, not anything else.

Victor peered over Paul's shoulder. "Couldn't we paint the walls of the parking structure with wild colors and create a friendlier atmosphere?"

Paul knew Victor wanted his approval. Since he'd worked with Victor in the past, he felt a loyalty to him. He'd promised the library job to him. Now, because of his love for Danielle, he regretted his decision.

Before Paul could force out a lame comment, Mr. Harrington spoke. "I'm not certain I like the idea of parking cars on the first floor of my library. What do you think, Paul?''

He felt as if the waiting room walls were crushing in on him. He'd planned to tell Mr. Harrington about Danielle. He'd planned to get the job for her. But he'd failed, and his mind and heart were ready to explode.

''Mr. Harrington, you'll have to excuse me,'' he apologized. ''I'm not feeling too well.''

Mr. Harrington looked concerned. ''Go home, Paul. I'll call you from San Francisco.''

In his van, Paul leaned his forehead against the steering wheel. He'd failed in the most important venture of his life—his relationship with Danielle. The honeymoon house didn't matter. The library didn't matter. All he cared about was that he was losing the only woman he'd ever loved.

In the construction trailer, Danielle anxiously grabbed her clothes out of the chest of drawers in the bedroom and threw them into her suitcase. Lisa had dropped her off at the trailer and promised to return in a little while to help her move her stuff back to their apartment.

Danielle tried to pack as quickly as possible. She needed to get out of the trailer before Paul got back. She didn't want to see him. She didn't want to hear his excuses about why he'd put his business before their love.

Her heart ached as she set her hand mirror, hair clips and perfume into her bag.

There'll be another children's library, she silently told herself. But she knew her promise to her parents had been annihilated. And the man she loved and trusted had helped destroy it.

She hurried into the bathroom to get her toothbrush. She accidentally picked up Paul's toothbrush. She felt the lump in her throat grow to grapefruit-size proportions. She thought she and Paul were a couple. A complete entity. Totally for each other. How foolish she had been.

Paul Richards cared about one person. Himself. His career. His life.

She put down his toothbrush and picked up her own, then spotted her filled laundry bag in the corner of the bathroom. The drawstring was open. On top of the pile of her clothes was Paul's T-shirt. She picked it up and smelled the manly scent of him on the fabric.

He'd mistakenly stuck his laundry in with hers. Or had he? Maybe he'd seen them as a twosome just as she had. But if he had, he would never have gone against her and supported another architect for his own personal gain. He would have fought for her. For them.

Suddenly, she heard the trailer door open. She gripped Paul's shirt between her fingers. Her heart thumped in her chest as she realized it was Paul.

# Nine

Paul stood in the trailer office, feeling as though his insides were being squeezed in a vise. Danielle's suitcases were packed. Her shopping bags were filled with her belongings. She was ready to leave his life for good.

Just then, Danielle came out of the bathroom. Her eyes were bloodshot. Her hair was mussed. His heart lurched as he realized the pain he'd put her through.

With trembling hands, she handed him a shirt. "You accidentally put your shirt in my laundry bag."

As he took the garment, his fingers touched hers. "Danielle, won't you give me a chance to explain?"

She quickly slipped her hand from his. "I—I need to finish packing."

She unplugged her computer, then picked up a computer disk from the table. He saw her eyes filling with tears. He realized that her sketch for the children's library was on the disk.

"Danielle, please don't give up what we have."

"Me?" she said, staring at him in disbelief. "You're the one who thinks 'single.'"

"Yeah, I used to—before we met, but now—"

"Paul, you don't know how to love," she cut in, putting the disk back down on the table. "You can't think in terms of being a couple. You're only out for yourself. You're never going to change."

Her words ripped through him like a sharp razor blade. "You're wrong, Danielle."

They were interrupted by a knock at the trailer door. Lisa entered. "Danielle, are you finished pack—" She stopped in midsentence as she looked from Danielle to Paul. "I can come back in a few minutes if you want."

"No," Danielle hurriedly said. She handed her sister a suitcase. "I'm ready to go home."

Outside the trailer, Danielle's heart was bleeding as she carried her shopping bags and suitcases to the car. After living with Paul, she'd never pictured returning to her apartment again. She'd fantasized that after the honeymoon house was finished she and Paul would get married and stay together forever.

How wrong her vision was.

As she loaded her car and Lisa's trunk with her belongings, Paul came out of the trailer, carrying her computer.

"If you don't have room in your car," Paul said, "I can bring this over in my van."

"No, thanks," she said swiftly, avoiding his eyes. "It'll fit in Lisa's trunk."

She didn't dare have him come to her apartment. Having him in her home would only remind her how much she'd wanted him to be the permanent man in her life.

The familiar roar of Butch's approaching motorcycle sent a tinge of agony through her body. Construction of the honeymoon house was over. And so were she and Paul.

Butch got off his bike and headed over to her. "Danielle, I'm gonna miss ya," he said, extending his hand for a shake.

"Butch, I hope we get to work together again." Then she hugged him, saying goodbye.

As Lisa started up her car, Danielle got into her own. She glanced back at the house. Her heart ached as she remembered when she and Paul had made love in the master bedroom, pretending it was their home.

Her gaze locked with Paul's. Was he remembering their lovemaking, too? If he'd really loved her, would he have put aside their love and crushed her dream of working on the children's library?

She forced her eyes from Paul and drove away.

Watching Danielle leave his life, Paul felt as though his heart were being yanked out of his body.

A huge truck arrived to haul the construction trailer from the site. He hurried back in the trailer to pack his stuff.

Inside, Paul spotted Danielle's computer disk lying on the table. She'd forgotten to take it. He quickly slipped the disk into his pocket. Butch helped him load his van without saying a word about him and Danielle.

As the truck driver hooked the trailer to the cab, Paul saw his intimate moments in the trailer with Danielle being torn from him.

Unable to watch any longer, he walked to the back of the honeymoon house. He stood near the cliff, staring at the waves of the Pacific Ocean, trying to settle the emotional hurricane rushing through him.

The memories of Danielle splashing him in the sea and losing her bikini top burned through his brain. The majestic ocean no longer sparkled knowing Danielle was no longer in his life. The blue sky didn't fill him with joy the way it had when she'd shared each day with him. Being alone used to feel normal to him. Now, after loving Danielle, he felt raw and unnatural.

Paul heard Butch gun up his motorcycle, reminding him that the honeymoon house job was finished. As he headed for his van, he reached inside his pocket for his keys and found Danielle's computer disk.

A spark of hope filled his being. He had an excuse to see her one last time.


At the flower shop, Danielle hoped that the hypnotic scent of roses, gardenias and carnations might momentarily make her forget the anguish of losing Paul and the library job. She was wrong.

Helping Lisa pick out their bouquets brought back the agony. She and Paul would never share the joy of getting married.

Lisa excitedly turned the pages of the flower brochure. "Danielle, should I get an all-gardenia bouquet?" She looked up when Danielle didn't respond. "You're thinking about Paul."

Danielle nodded. "I'm sorry, Lee. I don't want to spoil your wedding."

"Sometimes I wish I'd never gotten you that job," Lisa said.

"Don't say that," she instantly told her. "I loved working on the house."

Though she now ached inside, those days and nights with Paul had been the most beautiful of her life.

"Danielle, don't worry, something wonderful will happen to you," Lisa went on. "Maybe it'll be at my wedding. You'll get to meet Manny's best man. Manny says his friend is handsome and very, very single."

Danielle felt a cold emptiness in herself. "Don't go matching me up with anybody." No man could replace Paul.

"I just want you to be happy, Danielle."

"I know." She gave Lisa a hug and then quickly turned the pages of the flower brochure to get her mind off Paul. "Here's a beautiful arrangement for you, Lee." It was an exquisite bridal bouquet of fresh gardenias and tiny white roses. "What do you think?"

"Oh, yes!" Lisa squealed. "And I want you to carry one of miniature white roses to match mine!"

As Lisa ordered the two bouquets, Danielle spotted a fallen red rose petal on the floor. She gently picked it up and rubbed her finger on the satiny petal.

Without Paul, she felt disconnected, just like the lonely rose petal. Paul had brought a joy she never knew existed to each day. Why couldn't he have put their love first? Why?

Danielle tenderly set the rose petal down on the counter next to the vase of long-stemmed red roses and hurried out with her sister.

At his cottage, Paul slipped Danielle's disk into his computer. Before he took it back to her, he wanted to see her hard work once more. Her design for the children's library appeared on the screen.

Paul's eyes widened in awe as he stared at the exterior parking lot and three-story library. She had changed the design. Danielle's idea was far superior to Victor's.

He pulled out the disk from the computer. He wasn't going to return it to Danielle. He needed to show her plan to Mr. Harrington. Because without Danielle in his life, his partnership with Mr. Harrington suddenly had no meaning at all.

Paul picked up the phone right away and called Mr. Harrington's office, knowing he was still in San Francisco. He left a message with the secretary for Mr. Harrington to call him as soon as possible.

A couple of moments passed, when his phone rang. He yanked up the receiver, anxious to tell Mr. Harrington what he should have told him a long time ago about Danielle.

His old buddy bellowed over the line.

"Hey, Skip, when do I get to see you?"

"Lucky, are you back in L.A.?" He had wanted Danielle to meet his best friend. He had wanted to share his entire past with her. Now he was on his own again.

"I'm jetting into LAX tomorrow morning," Lucky replied. "We've got a lot of catching up to do."

When Paul finally hung up, he was plagued with mixed emotions. He couldn't wait to see his old friend. Yet without Danielle, he felt an emptiness that no one but her could fill.

To cheer himself up, he decided to surprise Lucky at the airport. He wished Danielle could go with him. Just the two of them. Arm in arm, in love.

Instead he'd be going it alone.

Still in the bed the next morning, Danielle felt someone touching her arm. "Paul," she whispered, thinking she was still in the construction trailer.

"Danielle, you've got to get up!" Lisa urged.

Danielle opened her eyes, realizing she wasn't in the trailer. And Paul wasn't with her. A deep sadness washed over her.

"A client just called and wants me to show her a property," Lisa said, rushing on. "Can you meet Manny at the airport and ask him to wait for me? I'll get there as soon as I can."

Danielle immediately sat up in bed. "Get to work," she said. "I'll tell Manny you're on your way."

"Thanks, Sis," Lisa said. "And don't forget. Manny will be sleeping over at his friend's place until our wedding." Then she was gone.

As Danielle hurried out of bed, she realized that her nightie was a bit damp. She remembered dreaming about Paul last night. She was with him in the master bedroom of the honeymoon house. His powerful body was moving sensually on top of hers. Her skin was still feverish from Paul's touch in her dream.

She took a shower to cool down and got dressed. She went to the refrigerator for orange juice, and saw Paul's hammer magnet on the door.

Her eyes clouded. She took the magnet off the door and

squeezed the cool metal in her palm. *Paul, how could you put aside our love for a business partnership?* she thought.

She should have discarded Paul's magnet and ended the memory of him right then and there. But she couldn't. Her heart was still in the way. She slipped the magnet into her bag and left for the airport.

Los Angeles Airport was bustling with taxis, hotel mini-buses and pedestrians as Paul entered the terminal to meet his childhood friend.

He tried not to, but he kept noticing couples in love, walking together hand in hand, or couples kissing as one parted from the other. Why couldn't one of those couples be him and Danielle?

*Because you can't keep love in your life,* he told himself.

He successfully went through the metal detecting machine and hurried toward the terminal where Lucky's plane was scheduled to arrive.

As he passed an airport shop, he suddenly stopped walking. Inside the shop, he saw Danielle standing by the magazine rack with her back to him.

His heart hammered against his ribs. He stepped into the shop and neared the magazine rack. He could smell the floral scent of her. He ached to caress her, to touch her velvety hair.

"Danielle," he whispered.

When Danielle heard Paul's deep voice behind her, she felt her fingertips immediately perspire on the magazine page. She looked up and felt blood rushing to her cheeks.

Paul was so close, she could reach out and touch his face. The love she felt for him surged from her heart to every muscle of her body. But she couldn't allow herself to give in to her emotions. She remembered that he'd yanked away the one dream she'd promised her parents.

"Paul, what're you going here?" she asked in a trembly voice.

"I'm having a reunion with an old friend of mine," he replied. "And you?"

His masculine voice. His charcoal eyes. All of him made her want him all over again.

"I'm meeting Lisa's fiancé," she told him. "The plane's late. Lisa's supposed to be here any minute, too." *I wanted to invite you to the wedding,* she yearned to add.

"Danielle, I know you don't want to talk to me—"

Despite the emotions that rose up in her, Danielle noticed passengers emerging from Manny's flight into the terminal.

Before Paul could continue, she cut in, "Paul, I've got to go." She tore herself away from him to look for Manny.

Through the thick crowd, she spotted Manny, wearing jeans and a jade shirt and holding two carry-on bags. He was searching the jammed terminal for Lisa.

Danielle tried to maneuver through the just-arrived passengers from other planes to get to Manny. Amid the throng of people, she saw Lisa reach Manny before her and fly into her future husband's arms.

As she tried to ease through the crowd to reach them, she bumped smack into Paul.

His strong hands were on her shoulders. His eyes were locked on hers. She was suddenly oblivious to everyone around her but him. She stared at him, wanting him to be the giving, supportive man she'd fallen in love with, not the man who'd been a traitor to their love.

"Danielle!" she heard Lisa call out.

Lisa and Manny were hurrying toward her. Just as Manny gave Danielle a warm hug, he turned to Paul with a broad smile.

"Hey, man, you're here!" Manny said excitedly. "Lisa, Danielle, I want you to meet my best man."

Danielle's mouth dropped open in shock. "What?"

Lisa glanced at Manny in utter dismay. "Your childhood friend is Paul?"

"Paul? I never call him 'Paul,'" Manny said, exchanging high fives with Paul and then bear-hugging him. "He's 'Skip' to me."

"Great seeing you, Lucky!" Paul said, his eyes meeting Danielle's.

Danielle couldn't breathe. She needed fresh air. She couldn't be the maid of honor at Lisa's wedding. Not when Paul Richards would be the best man!

In the airport parking lot, Paul's heart soared as he helped his friend put his luggage into his van. His best buddy had definitely brought him luck. Now he'd have a chance to be with Danielle a little longer because of the wedding. Maybe he could talk to her. Maybe she'd listen to him.

Paul glanced back at Danielle as she walked behind with Lisa, and tried to catch her eye. But she hastily looked away. His hopes dimmed. He knew he deserved her turning away from him. He'd injured her deeply. How could he expect her to trust him again?

Manny kissed Lisa. "I'll drop off my stuff at Skip's."

"No more nicknames," Lisa playfully ordered. "You make us girls feel we're with two strangers. Don't they, Danielle?"

Danielle looked at Paul. "Definitely strangers," she said in a low, disappointed voice.

His heart sank as she turned from his gaze.

"Okay, okay, no more nicknames," Manny agreed. "And don't worry, Lisa. Paul and I will go rent our tuxes."

"Oh, Manny, I love you!" Lisa squealed, kissing him again.

Paul yearned to hold and kiss Danielle just as Manny was doing with Lisa. But he knew she would never let him near her again.

Lisa grabbed Danielle's arm. "Come on. Manny and Paul will meet us later for dinner."

* * *

The moment Paul and Manny left in Paul's van, Danielle stared at her sister in utter disbelief. "I can't go to dinner with Paul."

"You've got to," Lisa said matter of factly. "You're my maid of honor. And Paul's our best man and Manny's dearest friend."

"Don't do this, Lisa," she pleaded. She was trying to forget Paul. But how could she if he was constantly near her?

Lisa frowned. "Dinner with the four of us is part of my wedding plans. You've got to get used to Paul's being around for the next few weeks."

Danielle felt helpless. She couldn't ruin the most exciting time of her sister's life. "Okay, okay," she finally said. "But the second, the very second, your wedding ceremony is over, I never want to see Paul's face again."

Lisa studied her. "Are you sure, Danielle?"

She tried to unlock her car door. "Of course I'm sure." But she was so nervous at the thought of never seeing him again that she dropped her keys in a puddle of motor oil on the ground.

At his cottage, Paul anxiously set down Manny's luggage. He couldn't forget the upset look in Danielle's eyes when Lisa said they'd all be having dinner together later.

"You haven't changed, have you, Paul?" Manny asked as he took off his shoes and made himself comfortable on the sofa. "You're still afraid of love."

"What're you talking about?" Paul yanked open the refrigerator door and passed a soda to his buddy. "I know how to love."

"Oh, yeah?" Manny challenged. "Then why are you holding back with Danielle?"

"What do you know about Danielle and me?" he asked, surprised.

"Lisa whispered a few words to me at the airport."

Paul slammed the refrigerator door. "I hurt her, Manny. Now she doesn't want anything to do with me."

"Are you going to run away from her the way you ran away from your stepmother when you were a kid?" Manny asked.

His friend's words hit him hard in the gut. He stared out the window of his cottage at the lush Italian cypress trees. He'd never been able to hold on to love. Why would he be able to now?

"Do you love Danielle?" Manny asked, cutting into his thoughts.

His heart swelled as he considered her. "She's everything I've ever dreamed of in a woman."

"Then pursue her until she marries you." Manny hopped off the sofa. "We'd better go rent those tuxes or Lisa might call off our wedding!"

As Paul locked the door to his cottage, the word *married* kept echoing through his brain. If he did get Danielle to forgive him, could he ask her to marry him? A rush of anxiety filled his bones. He'd be devastated if Danielle said no to him. And that's exactly what he was sure she'd say.

That evening with Lisa, Danielle nervously drove her car into a parking space on Wilshire Boulevard near the Santa Monica Promenade. Tiny white lights glistened on the trees, and neon specialty shop signs lit up the walking path.

She stared out her car window at the couples strolling in and out of shops and cafés in the promenade. She ached, knowing none of those couples would ever be her and Paul.

Just then, she spotted Paul standing with Manny in front of Rose's Italian Restaurant, waiting for them. He was laughing with Manny. His eyes were twinkling. His body looked lean and muscular under his jeans and shirt. He exuded a warmth and caring that she could feel even while sitting in her car.

Paul would have been so perfect for her, except for one thing. He had never made a real commitment to her. He'd never promised to be with her forever. Maybe that was the reason it had been easy for him to risk her love and give her dream job to Victor Horton.

She anxiously turned to Lisa. "Lisa, please don't get mad at me, but I can't have dinner with you."

Lisa looked upset. "Danielle, you promised."

She felt torn. "How can I pretend I'm having a good time, when I don't want to be here?"

She saw Lisa's eyes meet Manny's across the street. Her sister's face lit up. She opened the car door. "I know you won't desert me, Danielle." Then she got out.

"Lee, wait!" Danielle called, but her sister was already across the street, in Manny's arms.

Her eyes suddenly caught Paul's. She felt a yearning in her heart that made her instantly look away.

*Stop loving him!* she told herself. *He's only concerned about his own happiness, not yours.*

A few moments later, her car door opened.

"Danielle," Paul began. "Aren't you coming?"

Her heart thumped. *Tell him you can't go!* Instead she heard herself say, "I'd better not keep Lisa waiting."

She told herself she was going to dinner for her sister, not Paul. But as she got out of the car, she felt unsteady on her feet with Paul's solid frame so close to her.

She hurried across the street to Manny and Lisa. She couldn't walk near Paul and feel his intense presence beside her. She might weaken. She might forget that he was incapable of making a commitment to her.

Inside the restaurant, Paul pulled out a chair for Danielle. He smelled her sweet perfume as she sat down. Her raven hair was inches from his fingertips. He remembered caressing those soft strands in the honeymoon house. Now she didn't want him touching her at all.

As he sat next to her at the round table, he noticed

Manny caressing Lisa's neck and then nuzzling her earlobe. Lisa moaned and giggled.

Paul shifted uncomfortably in his seat and glanced at Danielle. She was nervously toying with the silverware on the table. He remembered how soft and warm her hand felt in his. He ached to reach across and close his palm over hers.

Instead he clasped his hands on the table.

He couldn't eat his dinner. He couldn't eat his dessert. He was too painfully aware of Danielle talking to Lisa and Manny. He felt she was deliberately ignoring him. He couldn't stand being shut out of her heart.

When the waitress brought the check, he picked up the tab before Manny could. He wanted to get the dinner paid for so he could grab a moment alone to talk to Danielle.

As he reached for his wallet, Danielle rose from the table. "I'm going to the powder room. I'll meet you all outside."

Danielle practically dashed away from the table. She felt tortured sitting next to Paul and not having his arm around her or his hand in hers. And seeing the love and affection between Lisa and Manny tormented her because she knew she'd never have that kind of love with Paul.

Just as she reached the ladies' room door, she felt Paul's hand grab hers.

"Danielle, please wait," he begged.

His palm was warm against hers. His intense eyes connected with her soul. All the love and closeness she felt for him at the honeymoon house came back. But the house was finished, and her fantasy about Paul was over, too.

"Paul, we have nothing to talk about."

His voice cracked. "How long are you going to hate me?"

Her heart wrenched. "I don't hate you." She wanted to yell out, I love you, Paul. But she couldn't let herself be that vulnerable with him again.

Paul gently squeezed her hand. "Danielle, don't you understand? I didn't know how badly you wanted the library job until it was too late."

It's not only the library job, she wanted to tell him. You're hooked on being single.

"Paul, I don't want to talk about the children's library."

"Danielle, I miss you."

His words tore at her emotions. She quickly released her hand from his and rushed into the ladies' room.

Once inside, Danielle nervously struggled to find her lipstick. Her bag slipped out of her hand and fell to the tiled floor. Her wallet, brush, pen, pad and lipstick tumbled out. Paul's hammer magnet glistened under the fluorescent light.

Oh, Paul, she silently groaned. She picked up his magnet and held the metal tenderly in her hand.

She hadn't meant to hurt Paul in the restaurant. But with his hand squeezing hers as though they belonged together, and the powerful feelings of closeness radiating between them, she had to pull away.

No matter how much she loved him, her heart was still burning from the way he'd turned his back on her for his own career needs. She quickly put his hammer magnet back into her bag and hurried out of the rest room.

In the crowded promenade, Danielle spotted Paul, Manny and Lisa near a jazz quartet playing music. Lisa and Manny were whispering to each other urgently. It almost looked as though they were quarreling. Paul was standing apart from them.

Once again, her impulse was to be with Paul. Just her and him. But instead she hurried over to Lisa and whispered in her ear, "I need to go home. Can Paul drive you and Manny back?"

Lisa looked anxious. "Danielle, I need to talk to Manny alone. I was hoping we could borrow your car."

"How will I get home?"

"I'll drive you," Paul said from behind her.

She felt trapped. She was afraid to spend another moment with Paul. Yet she sensed that Lisa was troubled and needed to speak to Manny.

"Sure, thanks," she forced herself to say to Paul.


Driving in his van, Paul glanced from crowded Wilshire Boulevard to Danielle in the seat beside him. She was staring out the front window. He'd caught her looking at him a few times since they'd left the Santa Monica Promenade.

He didn't want to take her straight home. He needed to be with her for just a little while longer.

"I know you want to get home," he began hesitantly, "but can I show you something first?"

Her turquoise eyes met his, and she wavered. "Okay."

Paul didn't know why, but he found himself driving to his old neighborhood in Santa Monica. He pointed to a beige house on the corner. "Manny used to live in that house."

"Where did you live?" Danielle asked.

As he neared the small gray house he'd grown up in, he slowed. Somehow having Danielle at his side made it easier to be near his painful past.

He parked his van one house away. "There's where I grew up." He felt a lump deep in his throat.

"What a cute place." Danielle leaned forward in her seat. "Who's the woman sitting at the window?"

Paul saw her, too. His fingers tightened around the steering wheel. His impulse was to leave. "My stepmother," he replied in a low voice. "I haven't seen her since I ran away when I was seventeen years old."

Danielle stared at him in surprise. "Why?"

He stared straight ahead. "After my father died, my stepmother was into her own kids. I was the outsider. I was the one in her way."

She touched his shoulder. "Paul, I'm sorry." The

warmth of her hand momentarily settled his hurricane of emotions.

"It's all in the past," he said, but he knew it wasn't. He knew his stepmother's rejection would always remain in his memory.

Danielle stared at the woman sitting at the window. "You haven't talked to her in so long. Why don't you knock on her door and say hello?"

Paul shook his head. "She probably won't even remember who I am."

"How do you know?"

"I don't think so."

Danielle opened her door. "Come on. I'll go with you." She got out. "Are you coming?"

Paul was wary. He had always been alone where his stepmother was concerned. Now Danielle was with him. Maybe he could face his past once and for all.

Danielle walked beside him as he approached the old house he used to live in. At the front door, he hesitated about ringing the doorbell.

"Maybe we can come by another time," he said.

Danielle pushed the button for him. "She's your only family, Paul."

His stomach tensed. He dreaded seeing his stepmother's cold, unwanting stare.

Suddenly, the door opened. An elderly woman with wrinkles around her eyes gazed at him for a long moment.

"Paul?" the woman began unsurely. "Is that you, Paul?"

Paul swallowed. He was surprised when Danielle grabbed his hand. A jolt of courage rushed through him. "Yeah, it's me," he forced himself to say.

His stepmother covered her mouth in shock. "Paul, where have you been all this time?"

"Just around," he replied, squeezing Danielle's hand, needing her with him more than ever.

His stepmother glanced over at Danielle. "Is this your wife?"

He noticed Danielle's cheeks redden. She gently released his hand and extended it to his stepmother. "I'm Danielle Ford, Paul's friend."

His stepmother warmly shook her hand. "Please come in."

Paul glanced at Danielle unsurely. He didn't want to drag her into this, but she just smiled at him and followed his stepmother inside.

# Ten

The living room was cluttered with piles of old newspapers. Dust covered the television set. His stepmother's tattered slippers were lying under the coffee table, just as they had when he was a kid.

"I know why you ran away, Paul," his stepmother said.

Paul tensed his jaw muscles. "We don't have to talk about this."

"I want to," she insisted. "I thought about it over and over until I couldn't think anymore." She stopped talking for a moment, as though it was difficult for her to speak. "It was my fault, Paul. I know how callously I treated you after your father died."

His anxiety increased. "Let's forget it, okay?"

Danielle slipped her arm through his, as if she knew he was struggling within himself. He could feel her love like a healing force inside him.

"I can't forget what I did to you, Paul," his stepmother went on. "Your father's death—leaving me alone with three children—it was too much for me. Even though I loved you, I took out my frustrations on you. I never meant to hurt you, Paul. Will you ever forgive me?''

Paul's hands felt ice-cold. All the torment of being rejected by her seared his bones. But Danielle squeezed his arm. She looked into his eyes as if she could feel his anguish, as if silently telling him that it was all okay now.

Without thinking, Paul put his arms around his stepmother, and for the first time in his life, he hugged her. And the warmth filled his soul.

''Can we still be a family, Paul?'' she asked. ''Will you come to see me again?''

Paul hesitated, but Danielle smiled and nodded at him once again, as though silently telling him that he didn't have to run away anymore.

''I'll visit whenever you want,'' Paul told her.

''The next time you come, Paul,'' she added with a twinkle in her eyes, ''you'd better bring your lovely friend with you.''

Paul glanced uneasily at Danielle. ''Well, I—''

Danielle warmly shook his stepmother's hand. ''I'd love to come.''

Driving Danielle home in his van, Paul felt a sense of elation and emotional freedom he'd never experienced before. And it was all because of Danielle.

''Thanks for being with me,'' he said, glancing over at her. ''I never would've gone into my stepmother's house if it hadn't been for you.''

''I never knew how far away you felt from your family,'' Danielle began. ''How lonely you must have been all these years.''

''I got used to it.'' But at that moment, Paul realized that he wasn't used to it anymore. He didn't want to be alone anymore. He felt a deep yearning to be with Danielle. Not just for a few minutes, but forever.

As he neared her apartment complex, he tried to find the words to tell her how he felt about her. But just as he

was about to speak, Danielle suddenly had a worried look
on her face.

Through the front window of Paul's van, Danielle spotted Lisa bursting out of her car, crying and running into
their apartment. Manny stood by her car, looking helpless.
She remembered that Lisa and Manny had been arguing
at the Santa Monica Promenade.

"Paul, stop the van!" she called.

Paul screeched to a halt. She got out of his van, with
him right behind her.

"Danielle, you talk to Lisa," Paul said. "I'll take care
of Manny."

She glanced back at Paul. She had the sudden feeling
that she and Paul were a solid couple, that something had
changed inside him after seeing his stepmother. She felt
that their relationship had real strength now.

In her apartment, Danielle found Lisa lying on the sofa,
crying. She sat down beside her and handed her a tissue.
"Lee, what happened?"

Lisa looked up with red, swollen eyes. "I called off our
wedding."

"Why?"

She wiped her nose. "Manny and I were talking about
having kids," she explained. "I told him I wanted to get
pregnant right away, but he said he didn't want to be a
father yet. He wanted to wait two or three years so he
could move ahead in his job." Her eyes brimmed with
new tears. "How can I marry him, when he's only thinking
about his needs and not mine?"

Lisa's words hit a familiar chord in Danielle. Wasn't
that the way she felt about Paul and the children's library?
"Lee, are you thinking about Manny's needs now or just
your own?" Hadn't she refused to recognize Paul's needs?
Hadn't she concentrated on her dreams and not his?

Lisa's eyes widened. "But Manny's needs are totally
opposite to mine."

"Are they?" Danielle asked. "If you look more closely, you might see that Manny wants exactly what you do, except not as quickly."

Paul kept flashing into her mind. In the honeymoon house, hadn't he said he loved her? Hadn't he said he needed her? Maybe when she'd wanted him to make that final commitment to her, he just hadn't been ready.

Lisa sat up on the sofa. "I don't know what to do, Danielle."

"Can't you see how lucky you are?" she went on. "You and Manny love each other. And your love makes you best friends above anything else. You can get through any problem together."

"Do you really think we can work it out?"

Danielle took her sister's hands in hers. "Talk to Manny. And don't stop listening to him. I know you'll both reach a compromise."

"What if it's too late?" Lisa asked, panicking. "What if Manny won't come back to me? Do you think Paul will encourage him to marry me?"

Danielle swallowed, at a loss what to say. She was aware of Paul's feelings about marriage. "Don't worry, Lee. Manny loves you. He'll come back."

Lisa hugged her. "Oh, I hope so!"

Danielle held her sister, sure of one thing. She'd done with Paul exactly what she'd told Lisa not to do with Manny. She'd refused to really *listen* to Paul's side of what had happened with the library job. She had forgotten that she and Paul were friends first and lovers second.

In his cottage, Paul watched Manny pace the living room. "Okay, so Lisa doesn't want to marry me. So what? Maybe I should stay single. You're not married, and you're happy."

Paul's muscles tensed. "You're wrong."

Manny stared at him, flabbergasted. "I thought living solo was the only mode of life for you."

Paul nervously ran his fingers through his hair. "It is—I mean, it was."

"Which is it?" Manny asked, confused.

"Listen, Manny," Paul began, the words flowing out before he could think about them. "When you find a woman you adore with all your soul, she becomes a vital part of you, like your brain and lungs."

That's what happened with me and Danielle, he wanted to say. Life without her was like losing the blood and oxygen in his body.

"But Lisa doesn't want me anymore," Manny complained.

Paul handed him the telephone. "You've got problems with Lisa? Solve them. Don't run away from your own heart."

Manny grabbed the phone. "You're right. What the heck am I doing letting her slip away from me?" He immediately dialed Lisa's number.

Paul knew what he had to do, too. He glanced at his answering machine. Mr. Harrington had left a message for Paul to meet him at his Century City office in the morning.

He took out Danielle's computer disk from his desk drawer. He was ready to risk everything for her. His business would survive with or without Mr. Harrington. But he couldn't imagine existing another day without Danielle.

In her kitchen, Danielle handed the telephone to Lisa. "It's Manny."

"He still loves me!" Lisa squealed as she hugged the phone to her ear.

Danielle went into the bedroom, wondering what Paul had said to Manny about love and marriage. Had he changed his viewpoint about making an emotional commitment?

She opened her closet to get ready for bed. Her gaze fell on her royal-blue maid-of-honor gown. As she fingered the elegant lace, she fantasized about Paul taking her into his arms at Lisa's wedding and asking her to marry him. Was it possible? Or was the idea of Paul proposing a crazy illusion?

She quickly closed her closet. But what if Paul's lifestyle was ingrained in him as strongly as family life was in her?

She sat down on her bed. How was she going to get through Lisa's wedding with Paul by her side? All she'd be thinking about was Paul and imagining him proposing to her.

Standing in Mr. Harrington's private office, Paul could feel his stomach was in a tight knot. Mr. Harrington sat at his desk, looking at Victor Horton's blueprints for the library. Paul protectively touched Danielle's computer disk in his pocket.

"Paul, I've studied Victor's revised parking structure," Mr. Harrington began, "but I still haven't arrived at a satisfactory decision."

Paul nervously took out Danielle's disk from his pocket. "Mr. Harrington, I have a solution for you."

He anxiously slipped the disk into the computer. His heart was pounding. On the screen, Danielle's sketch of the three-story library with the exterior parking lot appeared.

Mr. Harrington moved closer to the monitor. "What an incredible design. Why has Victor been hiding these plans from me?"

"This isn't Victor's."

Harrington looked confused. "What do you mean?"

Paul took a deep breath. "Mr. Harrington, I know Victor Horton is part of our business deal, but I don't think he's the right architect for your project."

"Then who is?"

"Danielle Ford," Paul firmly replied.

Mr. Harrington stared at her library plan. "This is Danielle's design?"

Mr. Harrington's positive response sent a surge of energy through Paul. "Danielle's greatest dream is to be the architect of a children's library. Your library, Mr. Harrington." Before Harrington could speak, Paul rushed on. "Mr. Harrington, I believe Danielle's plans are far superior to Victor Horton's."

There, he'd said it. His hands were sweaty. His shirt was moist. He'd risked ruining the three-way business partnership he'd arranged. But at that moment, it didn't matter. Danielle filled his heart. He wasn't going to ever let her down again.

On the day of Lisa's wedding, the white stretch limousine pulled up in front of the church. The chauffeur got out and held open the door for Danielle. She nervously stepped out in her gown, her bouquet of miniature roses in hand.

She anxiously scanned the front steps of the church, searching for Paul in the crowd of well-wishers. Stop thinking about him! she scolded herself. But Paul filled her every thought. She realized he was waiting inside the church with Manny.

She sucked in her breath as Lisa emerged from the limousine in her snowy lace wedding gown, carrying a bouquet of white gardenias and miniature white roses. A filmy white veil waterfalled over her blushing face.

"You look like an angel," Danielle whispered to her sister as tears clouded her eyes. "I wish Dad were here to walk you down the aisle."

"Dad would be proud knowing you were taking his place," Lisa whispered back.

Danielle followed Lisa into the church foyer. Sunlight streamed through the stained-glass windows, creating a kaleidoscope of colors.

As the wedding photographer adjusted the train of Lisa's gown for the pictures, Danielle peeked through the foyer doors into the church. Each pew was decorated with white gardenias to match Lisa's bouquet.

Danielle's gaze immediately fell on Paul as he stood at the bottom steps of the altar with Manny. She sucked in her breath at how handsome he was in a black tuxedo with crisp white shirt and black bow tie. Though she struggled not to, for a split second she wished that she were the bride and Paul the groom.

Just then, melodious organ notes of "The Wedding March" filled the church, alerting the guests that the bride was about to enter.

"Danielle, I'm so nervous!" Lisa whispered.

"Don't be," she whispered back. "Manny's waiting for you."

Danielle held tightly to her bouquet and strolled down the aisle beside Lisa. Though friends and acquaintances smiled at her and Lisa, Danielle saw only one person.

Paul was staring at her with awe in his eyes. Her legs felt weak. Her hands were trembling. She wished the priest were waiting to marry her and Paul.

Paul stood at Manny's side, unable to take his eyes off Danielle. She was the most beautiful woman he'd ever seen. Her blue gown accentuated her turquoise eyes. Her cheeks were pink, and her lips were painted the color of raspberries.

He was so wrapped up in Danielle that he could barely see Manny stepping to Lisa's side. He could barely recall walking up to the altar. He was engulfed in the love pouring out of his heart for Danielle.

The priest began. "Dearly beloved, we are gathered together in the sight of God to join Lisa Ford and Manuel Grant…"

Paul's eyes met Danielle's. Why wasn't he in Manny's place and Danielle in Lisa's? Why weren't the priest's words directed to him and Danielle? Did he still have a chance with her?

As the priest's prayers resonated through the church, Paul remembered his meeting with Mr. Harrington. Harrington had not told him the words he'd wanted to hear about hiring Danielle. Instead he had kept Danielle's computer disk and said he needed time to think about it.

Just then, Manny nudged Paul in the ribs, bringing him back to reality. "Paul, the rings!" Manny whispered.

Paul realized that the priest was waiting for him. He nervously reached into his pocket, then he handed Lisa's gold wedding band to Manny.

The priest intoned, "Do you, Manuel Grant, take Lisa Ford to be your lawfully wedded wife, to have and to hold…"

Paul watched his buddy slip the golden ring onto Lisa's finger and heard him say, "Yes, I do."

Paul looked over at Danielle. Her eyes were misty as she stared at him.

After Lisa put the matching gold wedding band onto Manny's ring finger, the priest said, "Manuel, you may kiss the bride."

Paul saw Manny lift the filmy white veil from Lisa's face and kiss his new wife. He realized that Manny wasn't just his best friend anymore. He was Lisa's husband now.

As Lisa and Manny left the altar, Paul noticed tears on Danielle's cheeks. He impulsively reached over and gently wiped away the droplets with his finger. He ached to draw her into his arms and ask the question that would seal their love. But would she say yes?

In the back seat of the white limousine on the way to the reception, Danielle joyously told her sister, "Congratulations, Mrs. Grant!"

"You're next!" Lisa excitedly said in return.

Danielle's cheeks flamed as she glanced at Paul and wondered if he'd heard. He was pouring champagne from the bar into four crystal glasses.

"To the beautiful bride and ugly groom!" Paul toasted with a playful grin at Manny.

"Wait till I get you at *your* wedding," Manny promised, eyeing Danielle.

Though Danielle was laughing, her heart was aching.

The moment the limousine arrived in Marina Del Rey, Lisa and Manny hurried onto the dock to their wedding yacht, where their guests were waiting.

As Danielle went to get out of the limousine, Paul touched her hand. "Don't go."

Her throat suddenly felt dry. "Lisa and Manny are waiting for us."

"You look beautiful, Danielle."

His deep, sensual voice. His warm, charcoal eyes. She was weakening inside. She was forgetting that Paul Richards wasn't the marrying kind.

His gaze drifted down to her lips. She wanted him to kiss her. Her skin ached to be caressed by him.

She leaned toward him, needing him, missing him, and just as his mouth was about to close over hers, she heard Lisa calling from the boat.

"Danielle! Paul! Come on!"

Danielle grabbed the bottom of her lace gown and hurried out of the limo. She ran toward the boat without turning back. Why had she let Paul see how much she still loved him, when after the wedding she'd never seen him again?

On the yacht, Paul searched for Danielle among the crowd of wedding guests who were laughing and conversing. He needed to talk to her. But how could he promise his love to her when he first needed to make up for the dream he'd taken away from her?

He went to look for a telephone. He had to find out Mr. Harrington's decision about hiring Danielle instead of Victor Horton.

He quickly dialed Mr. Harrington's office number. Mr.

Harrington had told him he'd be there working late to catch up after being in San Francisco.

When Harrington answered, Paul immediately said, "Mr. Harrington, I'm sorry to bother you, but—"

"Paul, I'm in a meeting with Victor Horton," Harrington cut in. "Can I call you back?"

Paul's hopes dropped. "I—I'll get back to you later, Mr. Harrington."

"By the way, Paul," Harrington continued. "Before my wife and baby return from San Francisco, I'd like to have you and Danielle over for lunch at my honeymoon house tomorrow afternoon. Will you relay my invitation to her?"

"Of course, Mr. Harrington."

Paul hung up, feeling that he'd failed. He'd desperately wanted to give Danielle what she desired most in her career. But Harrington had already made up his mind.

Paul stared at the crowd of wedding guests sipping champagne and wine. Tonight he wanted to tell Danielle that he needed to be with her always. But how could he? In a few weeks, he'd be going to the library job every morning without her. How could he leave her each day to work on a building he'd prevented her from designing?

The band on the boat warmed up. Danielle looked for Paul. Lisa and Manny were in the middle of the dance floor, ready for their first dance as husband and wife. Their eyes were aglow with love.

Danielle clasped her hands, feeling an overwhelming sadness. Where had Paul gone? Had she turned him away to the point where he'd left the wedding celebration before it had even begun?

The band started playing Lisa and Manny's favorite romantic ballad, "Until There Was You." Lisa and Manny went into each other's arms.

Couples joined Lisa and Manny on the dance floor. Danielle stood there, feeling very alone. No matter how much she fought her heart, Paul had become the other half of her. Without him at the wedding, she felt the urge to leave.

Just then, she sensed a familiar hand on her shoulder. "Can I have this dance?" Paul asked from behind her in that deep voice of his.

Her heart leaped. She turned around and looked up into Paul's warm eyes.

"I'd love to," she whispered.

The ballad resonated in her ears as Paul drew her into his strong arms and began to dance with her. His palm rested against the small of her back as he swayed with her. She circled both arms around his neck to get closer to him. But she felt Paul tensing against her.

"Mr. Harrington invited us over for lunch at his honeymoon house tomorrow afternoon," he said in a strained voice.

Her heartbeat quickened. The honeymoon house. That was why Paul felt anxious. Being there would only remind them that he'd recommended Victor Horton for the library job and not her. The children's library would always stand between them.

Just then, someone jostled her. She realized the band had switched to a fast song. Lisa and Manny were bumping and grinding next to them to the rock music.

Lisa grabbed Paul's hand and started dancing with him, while Manny became her partner, as the wedding crowd drifted between her and Paul.

Later, at the head table, Paul could barely eat the filet mignon. He yearned to be alone with Danielle. Ever since he'd brought up lunch at the honeymoon house with Mr. Harrington, she had withdrawn emotionally from him.

The four-tiered whipped-cream wedding cake was wheeled out on a cart. As Lisa and Manny fed each other cake, Paul's eyes met Danielle's. He wanted to be feeding her wedding cake—their wedding cake.

Just then, Manny grabbed Paul's arm. "Come on,

Paul!'' Manny said. ''I'm going to throw the garter to all you single guys!''

Before Paul could protest, he was standing in the middle of all the bachelors at the wedding. Manny flipped Lisa's powder-blue garter over his shoulder. Paul saw it fly high into the air. The lace garter landed in his hand. Cheers filled the hall.

Manny slapped him hard on the back. ''You're next!''

Paul was so filled with emotion that he didn't see Lisa throw her bridal bouquet to the crowd of single women. A moment later, he saw Danielle holding Lisa's gardenia bouquet. Her face was flushed. She looked radiant and soft. He nervously twirled the garter belt on his finger. What if he asked her, ''Will you be my wife?'' Would she say yes or turn her back to him?

Before Paul knew what was happening, Danielle was guided to sit on a chair in the middle of the dance floor, and he was pushed to follow.

''Paul, slip the garter on Danielle's leg!'' Lisa called out, laughing.

Paul's face was burning hot with embarrassment. He got down on one knee in front of Danielle and slowly lifted the hem of her royal-blue gown.

When he pushed her gown up to her knees, the wedding crowd yelled, ''Higher! Higher!''

Paul's eyes locked with Danielle's as he held the hem of her dress between his fingers. He pushed the dress higher up her thighs and then lifted her leg to slip on the garter.

His gaze traveled to the panty hose between her parted thighs. He swallowed hard when he realized she wasn't wearing any panties under the nylon.

He felt his body react and hoped no one noticed how turned on he was.

As he slid the garter over her ankle, Manny called out, ''Paul, no hands allowed! Use your imagination to get that garter onto her thigh!''

The wedding guests cheered Paul on. He leaned over and settled his mouth on the edge of the lace. Danielle's leg was trembling. He pulled the garter over her knee onto her midthigh.

Suddenly, he lost his grip on the hem of the gown, and the dress covered his head. He heard the crowd clapping at the fun of it all.

In those few seconds under Danielle's dress, Paul could smell the flowery scent of her. He was only inches from her womanliness. He could feel his manhood growing hard.

Just then, Danielle pulled up her dress, freeing him. His gaze met hers. Her eyes were glazed, and he knew she was as aroused as he was.

The wedding band started playing a rock song. The guests were dancing. Danielle felt Lisa grab her to sway to the beat. She turned to see Paul walking off with Manny's arm around his shoulder. She could still feel Paul's lips touching her inner thigh. The feminine area between her legs tingled. She ached to make love to him.

The wedding reception was over before Danielle realized it. She hadn't had a chance to be with Paul again. She drove Lisa back to their apartment to get her suitcase for her honeymoon to Hawaii. The rest of Lisa's belongings were already in the new house that she and Manny had rented before the wedding.

Before Danielle closed Lisa's suitcase, she slipped in the white filmy negligee she'd bought Lisa as a surprise for her wedding night.

"Enjoy your first evening as Manny's wife," Danielle said, giving her sister a warm hug.

"I'll miss you," Lisa whispered back.

"No, you won't," she said with a secret smile. "You'll be having too much fun with Manny!"

Manny's car horn out front signaled that he was anxiously waiting for his new bride. Danielle walked her sister to the door, trying not to get teary eyed.

"Danielle, I know I've forgotten something!" Lisa said worriedly.

"If you leave anything behind, I'll mail it to you in Hawaii." She gave her sister one last hug.

The moment Lisa left, the apartment rang of emptiness. The only person on her mind was Paul. She hadn't even said goodbye to him after the wedding.

In her bedroom, she shed her gown, panty hose and bra. She remembered dancing cheek to cheek with Paul at the wedding. In his arms, she'd felt that he was her man. Why wasn't he with her? Why weren't she and Paul going on their own honeymoon?

Her sadness was overwhelming as she slipped on a terry-cloth robe Lisa had left in their closet. She searched for the belt to the robe but couldn't find it.

Just as she was about to leave the bedroom, she spotted Lisa's makeup case and apartment keys lying on the floor between the twin beds. She picked up the keys and the case, frantically thinking of a way to get Lisa's case to her.

At that moment, she heard a knock at the door. She rushed to unlock the door, the makeup case in her hand.

"Lee, I knew you'd remember your makeup—"

Paul was standing there in his tuxedo. He was holding his bow tie. His starched white shirt was unbuttoned at the top. His gaze drifted down to the opening of her robe.

Her cheeks heated up. "I—I thought you were Lisa."

Paul cleared his throat. "I was driving past."

His husky voice resonated to her every nerve ending. "Come in," she said.

As Paul entered her kitchen, he frantically searched his mind about what he was going to say to her. Should he tell her, I tried to get you the library job, but I miserably failed at that, too?

But when Danielle closed the door and turned to face him, he stopped thinking. He stopped wondering. Her turquoise eyes blended with his. Her breathing came quickly. Her terry robe was still open at the front. He realized she was naked under the fabric.

Paul reached for the lapel of her robe and drew her to him. "I need you, Danielle," he heard himself say.

She held his face between her warm hands. "Paul, I love you so much!"

He crushed her to him. Her lips met his. He slipped his hands inside her robe and caressed her breasts.

She slipped off his tuxedo jacket, unbuttoned his shirt and shed his clothes, until he was naked against her. Sliding her robe off her shoulders, he lifted her off the floor and set her on the edge of the kitchen table.

He gently spread her legs and ran his hands up her inner thighs until his fingers reached her moist femininity. She moaned as he slipped his finger inside her. His body grew hot with desire as he felt her spasm with pleasure.

"Paul, I want to feel you inside me," she groaned.

He removed his finger and slid his aching manhood into the depths of her. "Danielle, Danielle—" he whispered over and over, submerging himself in her. "I love you."

As he thrust in and out of her, he felt as if he were floating through infinity with her. He never wanted to be separated from her again.

His masculinity expanded to explosive proportions. Then he groaned as his juices filled her. He opened his eyes and gazed into hers, watching their souls merge into one.

As their breathing subsided, he carried her to the bed and tenderly laid her down. She rested her face against his chest and a serenity enveloped him. There was no other place for him in the universe except beside her.

As the morning sun filled her bedroom, Danielle heard Paul's beeper go off. When she opened her eyes, he was already out of the bed. She could hear him talking on the phone in the living room.

She slid the blanket off her and sat up, then heard him saying Victor Horton's name.

"Sure, Victor," Paul agreed. "I can meet you in an hour or so."

Victor Horton. The children's library. Their lovemaking could never make that pain go away.

Paul walked into the bedroom. He had on his white shirt and tuxedo. His bow tie was hanging out of his pocket. She could see the worry in his eyes. He felt the strain between them, too. And there was no way he could ever make it go away.

"What time do you want me to pick you up to go to the honeymoon house?" he asked.

"I'll meet you there later," she quickly said, avoiding his gaze. "I've got a few things to do this morning."

In his van, Paul pushed down hard on the gas pedal as he zoomed down Danielle's street. He felt helpless. Last night, making love, then spending the whole night together, he'd felt as though he was married to her.

The words asking her to marry him were on the tip of his tongue. But how could he now? He'd seen the pain in her eyes after he'd spoken to Victor. She could never forget what he'd taken away from her. And neither could he.

*Face it*, he thought. *Danielle will never marry you.*

Danielle arrived at the honeymoon house a few minutes early. She was relieved that Paul's van wasn't there yet. She knew how tense they would feel together the moment Mr. Harrington brought up the children's library.

As she walked up to the door of the house, memories of her and Paul filled her mind. The house would always be an intimate part of her. It was her and Paul's work of love.

She pressed the doorbell. Mr. Harrington opened the front door to greet her.

"I'm delighted to see you, Danielle."

As she walked into the sunken living room, her heart ached. To her, the honeymoon house was Paul. The smell of wood. The perfectly shaped fireplace. The floor-to-ceiling window in the master bedroom. The entire construction. It was Paul who'd made her vision of the house come alive.

"Is the house comfortable for you, Mr. Harrington?" she asked, remembering how she and Paul had fantasized that the home was theirs.

"I enjoy every second of living here," Mr. Harrington replied. He motioned her into his study. "However, we must discuss your plan, Danielle."

"My plan?" she asked, confused. Had she forgotten to design a cabinet or closet he'd wanted?

Mr. Harrington turned on his computer. Suddenly, her design for the children's library appeared on the screen.

She stopped breathing. "How did you get—"

"Paul brought me the disk," Mr. Harrington replied. "Your children's library is perfect, Danielle."

Her heart beat faster. "But you already have a set of plans to work with."

"Yes, but Paul has done a superb job of convincing me that you are the best architect for my library," Mr. Harrington went on.

Danielle's knees felt weak. "What about Victor Horton?"

"I spoke at length with Victor last night at my office," he continued. "He has admitted that he doesn't have a feel for the library. Therefore, I have recommended him for a couple of large office buildings that a friend of mine is constructing."

Just then, the doorbell rang. "Paul is here," Mr. Harrington said as he left the study.

Danielle stared at her library design on the monitor. She

pinched herself to see if she was dreaming. Mr. Harrington loved her plan! And it was all because of Paul. He'd come through for her.

In the living room, Paul could barely contain his excitement at the news he'd just learned. He'd just come from Victor's apartment. Victor had told him about his new job with Mr. Harrington's friend. Paul had practically flown his van to the honeymoon house to see Danielle.

As Paul walked into the study with Mr. Harrington, Danielle rushed into his arms and hugged him.

"Thank you," she whispered. "I love you, Paul."

"I love you, too," he whispered back.

Mr. Harrington eyed them curiously and sat down at his desk. "I'm very satisfied with the great architect-contractor team I have to build my children's library." He took out a contract from his desk drawer. "Paul, I'm ready to sign my deal with you. However, I want to make one revision."

Paul's heart pounded. He couldn't believe he was finally getting his partnership! "What revision is that, Mr. Harrington?"

"I would like you and Danielle to work for me as a team, not only on my library but on all the commercial structures I plan to build in the future."

Danielle beamed. "Mr. Harrington, you want *me* to be the architect in your partnership with Paul?"

"Correct," Mr. Harrington replied. "Paul, how do you feel about working on a permanent basis with Danielle?"

Paul realized that his moment had come. "Mr. Harrington, I'll consent to your offer only on one condition."

"What do you have in mind, Paul?" Mr. Harrington asked.

"May I speak with Danielle privately for a few minutes?" Paul requested.

"Of course."

The moment Mr. Harrington left the study, Danielle turned in panic to Paul. "Why are you hesitating?"

He leaned against the desk. "Danielle, I have my own idea of what my partnership with Mr. Harrington should be."

She looked crushed. "Don't you want me in the partnership?"

He shook his head. "I can't work side by side with you twenty-four hours a day the way things are between us."

Frustrated, she glared at him. "Why do you always think about yourself? Can't you see what a great opportunity this would be for the two of us?"

"Danielle, we live in two separate worlds," he explained. "I want to work with an architect who'll share one world with me."

"What—what do you mean?" she stammered, unsure.

Paul swallowed, anxiety filling his body as he desperately hoped for the answer he yearned to hear. "Danielle," he said. "Will you be my wife?"

"You want to marry me?" she asked, incredulous. "Paul Richards? The man who wants to remain eternally single?"

Paul felt his spirits sink. "If you don't want to, Danielle, I'll understand—"

"Yes!" she cried, circling her arms around his neck. "I'll be your wife forever, Paul, forever."

His heart was pumping. "You will? You really will?"

Paul held Danielle close to him, unable to believe her yes. He was so thrilled and elated that he didn't hear Mr. Harrington return to the room.

Mr. Harrington cleared his throat. "Now, about our partnership deal."

Paul gently released her from his arms, but he couldn't take his eyes off his future bride.

"Mr. Harrington," Paul began in a hoarse voice. "Danielle and I accept your business proposal. And we want to invite you to our wedding!"

# Epilogue

Two months after her beautiful wedding to Paul, Danielle excitedly stood at the construction site of the children's library. She watched in awe as powerful steel girders were lifted by a huge crane to frame the library she'd promised her parents.

She spotted Paul standing on a beam, instructing the crane operator where to put down the steel girders. Her heart filled with love.

She couldn't believe that her two dreams had come true—the children's library and her marriage to Paul Richards. Now she had a third dream.

Lunchtime arrived. The crane was turned off. Butch and the crew headed off the property to eat their sandwiches.

Paul walked over and drew her against his perspiring, hard body. His manly scent immediately turned her on.

She grabbed his hand. "I've got a surprise lunch for you."

His eyes lit up as he followed her into the construction trailer. She locked the door and closed the window blinds. She lit the scented vanilla candle she'd set up on the table, where she had sandwiches already made.

She removed his tool belt and slowly unbuttoned his shirt. She slid her palms across his massive chest. He groaned and covered her mouth with his.

"Since ground broke on the library," she whispered, "I've counted the hours until our lunch together."

"Is this my surprise?" he asked, cupping her breasts in his hands.

She giggled. "Wait here. I'll be right back." She hurried into the bathroom.

Paul could barely let Danielle out of his sight because he wanted more of her. From the bathroom, he could hear the water running.

Feeling his stomach grumble with hunger, he took a piece of the tuna sandwich she'd made for him. Then he saw the small wrapped present on the table. His name was printed on it.

He smiled. Her surprise. He quickly unwrapped the gift. His heart swelled as he held a yellow baby rattle in his hand. A joy he'd never felt before filled his being.

In the bathroom, Danielle felt her hands perspiring. She was sure Paul had found her gift. She slowly opened the bathroom door. She was nervous about how he was going to react.

Paul walked over and tenderly touched her stomach. "Our baby?" he whispered. "I'm going to be a father?"

She nodded. "Is that okay, Paul?"

He opened his mouth to speak, but tears filled his eyes. She put her arms around him, and he held her silently for a long moment.

She knew Paul was as joyful as she was. Paul Richards. Her husband. The father of her baby. Yes, all her dreams had finally come true.

*     *     *     *     *

**They called her the**

# Champagne Girl

**Catherine:** Underneath the effervescent, carefree and bubbly facade there was a depth to which few had access.

**Matt:** The older stepbrother she inherited with her mother's second marriage, Matt continually complicated things. It seemed to Catherine that she would make plans only to have Matt foul them up.

With the perfect job waiting in New York City, only one thing would be able to keep her on a dusty cattle ranch: something she thought she could never have—the love of the sexiest cowboy in the Lone Star state.

**by bestselling author**

# DIANA PALMER

Available in September 1997 at your favorite retail outlet.

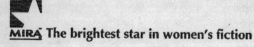

# Take 4 bestselling love stories FREE

## Plus get a FREE surprise gift!

## Special Limited-time Offer

**Mail to Silhouette Reader Service™**

3010 Walden Avenue
P.O. Box 1867
Buffalo, N.Y. 14240-1867

**YES!** Please send me 4 free Silhouette Desire® novels and my free surprise gift. Then send me 6 brand-new novels every month, which I will receive months before they appear in bookstores. Bill me at the low price of $2.90 each plus 25¢ delivery and applicable sales tax, if any.* That's the complete price and a savings of over 10% off the cover prices—quite a bargain! I understand that accepting the books and gift places me under no obligation ever to buy any books. I can always return a shipment and cancel at any time. Even if I never buy another book from Silhouette, the 4 free books and the surprise gift are mine to keep forever.

225 BPA A3UU

| | | |
|---|---|---|
| Name | (PLEASE PRINT) | |
| Address | | Apt. No. |
| City | State | Zip |

This offer is limited to one order per household and not valid to present  Silhouette Desire® subscribers. *Terms and prices are subject to change without notice.
Sales tax applicable in N.Y.

UDES-696                              ©1990 Harlequin Enterprises Limited

## ATTENTION
## ALL JOAN JOHNSTON FANS!

Silhouette Books is pleased to bring you two brand-new additions to the #1 bestselling Hawk's Way series—the novel you've all been waiting for and a short story....

**"Joan Johnston does contemporary westerns to perfection."** —*Publishers Weekly*

Remember those Whitelaws of Texas from Joan Johnston's HAWK'S WAY series? Jewel Whitelaw is all grown up and is about to introduce Mac Macready to the wonders of passion! You see, Mac is a virgin...and it's going to be one long, hot summer....

## HAWK'S WAY
## THE VIRGIN GROOM
August 1997

And in November don't miss Rolleen Whitelaw's love story, *A HAWK'S WAY CHRISTMAS*, in **LONE STAR CHRISTMAS**, a fabulous new holiday keepsake collection by talented authors Joan Johnston and Diana Palmer. Their heroes are seductive, shameless and irresistible—and these Texans are experts in sneaking kisses under the mistletoe! So get ready for a sizzling holiday season....

Only from

HWXMAS

## FANTASTIC NEWS!

For all you devoted Diana Palmer fans
Silhouette Books is pleased to bring you
a brand-new novel and short story by one of the
top ten romance writers in America

**"Nobody tops Diana Palmer...I love her stories."**
—*New York Times* bestselling author
**Jayne Ann Krentz**

---

**Diana Palmer has written another thrilling desire.
Man of the Month Ramon Cortero was a talented
surgeon, existing only for his work—until the
night he saved nurse Noreen Kensington's life. But
their stormy past makes this romance a challenge!**

### THE PATIENT NURSE
**Silhouette Desire**
October 1997

---

And in November Diana Palmer adds to the
Long, Tall Texans series with *CHRISTMAS COWBOY*, in
**LONE STAR CHRISTMAS**, a fabulous new holiday
keepsake collection by talented authors Diana Palmer
and Joan Johnston. Their heroes are seductive,
shameless and irresistible—and these Texans are
experts at sneaking kisses under the mistletoe! So get
ready for a sizzling holiday season....

Only from

# SILHOUETTE® *Desire*®

## 15 YEARS OF GUARANTEED GOOD READING!

Desire has always brought you satisfying novels that let you escape into a world of endless possibilities— with heroines who are in control of their lives and heroes who bring them passionate romance beyond their wildest dreams.

When you pick up a Silhouette Desire, you can be confident that you won't be disappointed. Desire always has six fresh and exciting titles every month by your favorite authors— **Diana Palmer, Ann Major, Dixie Browning, Lass Small and BJ James,** just to name a few. Watch for extraspecial stories by these and other authors in **October, November and December 1997** as we celebrate **Desire's 15th anniversary.**

Indulge yourself with three months of top authors and fabulous reading…we even have a fantastic promotion waiting for you!

**Pick up a Silhouette Desire… it's what women want today.**

Available at your favorite retail outlet.